The Sameness Life of Nandi

By

Memory Bengesa

The Sameness Life of Nandi

A Novel 2014 ©

ISBN 978-0-9995371-2-1

Copyright © 2018 by Memory Bengesa.

"So if the Son sets you free, you will be free indeed."

—John 8:36 ESV

CHAPTER ONE

The first week of January 2014, St Louis, Missouri

It had to be the coldest January afternoon on record. The icy January wind; bulged with disrespect, pierced through my veins as my soul wept in graveyard silence. The car ride home was the most silence my mind had ever embraced. What a difference from the last four years of automatic motion, the constant go-go-go. What complete chaos my life had been.

I knew that day was coming, but denial was easier than admitting the bold-faced truth. It's funny that I, of all people, had faith that God would spare her. Huh! God! Or the "higher power" or whatever you want to call Him. I thought He would allow her more time here on earth. After all, it would be for the benefit of His work, so she would say.

Sigh. "We're home, honey." Brian said.
I could hear his voice, but I couldn't hear his words. It didn't take much for me to snap back to reality the minute Brian opened my

door to help me out of the car. My body was hit by the cruel, icy wind that generally swept St. Louis in mid-January.

"Can I get you a cup of hot tea, babe?" Brian asked while assisting me with my coat.

"I just need to lie down." Suddenly weak, I walked slowly to the closest bedroom while Brian entertained the phone callers. I could not bear to talk or even hear my phone ringing. I knew that people intended no harm, all was just a humble response to customary obligations, but these calls would soon cut into my last nerve.

The last thing I wanted to hear at that tensed state was the predictable line, "we're sorry for the loss, they loved her, they are there for me and she will be missed, blah, blah, blah." As potentially comforting their sincere condolences might have sounded, it was detrimental to me in that state.

No one knows how much pain you go through at the loss of a loved one. I know I am guilty of it too. I was always uncomfortable at funerals, thinking I was saying comforting things. But truth be told, no amount of comforting is actually enough to comfort one who just lost a loved one. It's true that you don't know until you walk in the same shoes.

One of the perquisites that go along with being married to Brian is the comforting scent of security, stability, and protection I get to perceive every day. I needed no external force to tell me Brian had walked in, my nose had always been enough since our first date and always will be.

I knew he was there because I could smell his cologne, even through the congestion in my nose. He sat at my feet as I curled up in a fetal position in the bed. I could not stop crying—I just couldn't. I'd been strong throughout the whole process. In that moment, I just wanted to bawl like a little baby, because nothing could stop my emotions and pain—not Brian, not my concerned family or friends.

He rubbed my back gently, with a hint of authenticity and I began to long for his gentle strokes of comfort. "How could this gesture feel so brand-new and real to me in my state of grief?" I thought to myself. This touched my emotions deeper. I can't tell you the last time I felt Brian's authentic touch the way I felt that day. The touch was encapsulated with calculated doses of emotional freedom, as though it was summer time.

"Babe," Brian said softly. "Do you remember when we first met?"

I couldn't help but chuckle. Through all my pain and tears, this man knew how to put a smile on my face. "You stalked me until I agreed to go out with you." Brian couldn't keep a serious face if he tried.

"What?" he hollered.

"You heard me, Mr. Stalker."

"Well—Nandi, after twelve years of marriage, I guess my stalking paid off."

Sigh. "You did something right." I couldn't help but mumble that.

I couldn't believe it had been twelve years. They were not short years. They had more downs than ups. My feelings were reminders of those downs and ups, and my husband wouldn't like it if he knew I thought so.

"I'm going to get into some comfortable clothes and let you rest." Brian stood, kissed my forehead, and walked out.

I could feel him lingering at the door. My pain hurt him too. I knew he felt horrible because he couldn't immediately fix it as he would like to, being the problem-solver by nature. When the door shut, my mind strolled back to total darkness. A part of me knew that the best thing

for me to do was to think happy thoughts, but how do you emancipate yourself from mental slavery when you are combatting with such tragedy?

My mind felt like an out-of-control carousel. It fixated on one thought then another, then another, and then that thought went around and round. I tried to pray. Yes, if I was praying, that meant it was serious. But all I could think of was Brian and her, or her and Brian. My heart beat faster and faster. I squeezed my eyelids shut to wash out my thoughts, but the more I tried, the more I thought of the funeral. And when I tried not to think of the funeral, I thought of my personal loss.

My head felt heavier by the second. I was reaching meltdown stage at the worst possible moment, I wanted it all to disappear, so I could get back all the good memories of my life. Maybe the doctor's diagnosis was correct...

* * *

When I think of Momma Jean's love and passion for God, I have to wonder how she remained so faithful to God until her death. Her cancer came and went for almost four years, and right when we thought it was all gone, it came back with vengeance.

Momma Jean never smoked nor drank. She was a healthy-lifestyle activist. Her diagnosis of malignant cancer of the lungs was by far the most shocking news any of us had ever heard. What's crazy is that the day she told me about it, she had no tears in her eyes. That woman was a strong warrior. I was the one she had to control. I wept so much that one would have thought I was the patient. I remember her soft, cuddling voice. "Don't you worry, child. My God is able." Those were her favorite words. No matter how old I was, she still considered me a child. I guess some things never change.

A lot of unanswered questions went down six feet with Momma Jean—a lot of unanswered questions I was scared to ask. I never dwelt on the questions before she died, because I never wanted to be one of those children who grew up expecting a great outcome from the answers to my mother's past. For instance, I've never known who my biological father is—or was. I had many questions about my life, but ultimately, I wanted to know my father.

Never for one second did I consider asking Momma Jean who he was because she never made me thirst for any sort of paternal influence, she was there for me in literally everything that I almost didn't remember my father wasn't in the picture.

She worked two hard jobs just to keep a roof over our heads and to make sure I made it to medical school. She never missed a day of work in her life. So, in the midst of it all, I didn't want to disrespect her by bringing up a memory of her past, even though it was an important piece of who I was.

After I turned eighteen, I thought she'd tell me who my father was, but she didn't. I fought with the thought of asking her until I was able to wrap my brain around the fact that, telling me was entirely of her own coinage. I couldn't force her, even though I wanted to.

The years came and went, and now she was six feet underground. She could never reveal to me the other half of my identity. All I knew was that we moved to East St. Louis, Illinois, from Shuqualak, Mississippi, when I was ten.

I remember that myself. As for my childhood, it was interesting even though I never got to spend much time with Momma Jean. She worked two jobs and went to school, so the neighborhood pretty much raised me after we moved to Illinois. Amazingly, in those days, you could trust the neighborhood to do such things. Everyone on my block was an aunt or uncle but were no blood relation. They were free to discipline me if I was out of line.

What's crazy is that I don't remember ever meeting a blood relative in East St. Louis. I never thought to dwell on it, as my neighborhood and church had plenty of play-uncles and play-aunts and cousins. I didn't have much to compare my childhood lifestyle too. I could not have told you what a "normal" childhood looked like.

My life changed after my sixteenth birthday. We moved from East St. Louis out to the county across the bridge—or across the river, as some folks would say—to Missouri. There we enjoyed an upgraded lifestyle.

This new house had a working air conditioner and heat. I can't help remembering what a big difference it made during the winters and summers. In time, we even owned a fancy "ice-box," which I thought only the super-rich could afford. We'd never had one before. It took me a while to get used to the washer and dryer because in Mississippi and in East St. Louis, all we ever used was the washboard. What's funny about my growing-up years is that I never thought there was something called social upheaval. I never thought we were poor or without. Whatever I needed, Momma Jean got for me.

What we didn't have, I didn't know about. Only when we moved into a completely different and diverse neighborhood did I realize how other people lived. That realization taught me a different perspective. We were poor when we lived on Tudor Avenue in East St. Louis, compared to our new upgrade.

By the time we moved, Momma Jean was finally done with her Ph.D. and had landed her dream job as a professor in the department of African-American studies at a local college. In a funny sense, I missed that little brick house in East St. Louis because it was my refuge from Mississippi. I missed the people who made up the neighborhood, although we had the smallest duplex on that street.

Now my memories of Tudor Avenue, my friends, and my neighbors lay dominant in my head. That neighborhood was what raised me not to forget the little white brick building we called church. Momma Jean wouldn't let us skip a day of service, making sure she was always off work on Sundays. One time, she had a bad case of pneumonia, and the doctors tried unsuccessfully to place her on bedrest. We attended a church that Sunday, doctor or no doctor.

She had me later in life—in her second year of college. I got used to calling her Momma Jean because that's what the neighborhood kids called her, and their mothers called her Sister Jean. She never stopped me from calling her Momma Jean.

Amidst all the tension, a part of me was pretty angry at this God she'd stayed loyal to. Another part of me feared I hadn't done as much as I needed to do for her when she was in remission....

CHAPTER TWO

Thirty years earlier in Mississippi.

The year of my tenth birthday was sweltering hot, smack-dab in the middle of the Mississippi summer. I remember the sticky feeling of my sweat against my cotton clothing. I awoke to Momma Jean and Lois going at it in a whispered argument. I pressed my ear against the thin, chipped wall to hear as much as I could, as I always did. But the harder I pressed my ear to the wall, the softer they whispered. I had grown accustomed to their bickering, usually over petty stuff.

I didn't know what relation Lois was to Momma Jean, but I do know she was meaner than a three-legged dog. She was so mean that one needed not to spend a second with her before getting pissed; her smell was enough. I couldn't tell how old she was, but back in those days, she could have well been as old as Methuselah. At least, that's what I thought in my young mind because she looked so archaic. It

12

must have been the thinning coarse gray hair, crafted wrinkles on her face, and the unattractive pronounced frown lines on her forehead, representing both a hard life and endurance. Or the fact that she was one of the founding mothers at our little brick church might have made me feel she was ancient. Either way, I was not too fond of Lois.

Lois had a stoic-stern face and a raspy, loud voice. She was always on the grouchy side. If she'd ever had a smile on her face, I must have missed it. Whatever the case, she was related to Momma Jean closely, it seemed. She always told me to call her Lois or Miss West. Momma Jean never formally introduced us or acted for a second as if I needed to know who she was. She was just Lois West.

She took care of me when Momma was at work and school. Well, taking care of me is an exaggeration. But I can say Lois West did what she could to take care of me. I used to hear the neighborhood and church kids calling her Grandma L. One day, I called her Grandma L, just like the rest of the kids my age, and mind you, I called her Grandma L when she was cooking.

Boy! You would have thought I had insulted her.
She whirled around. "What did you call me, little girl?"
Her voice was so raspy, it terrified me. I looked down and whispered, "Grandma L." In an instant, she was across the room. She lifted my face, her palm tucked underneath my chin, and squeezed the nerve endings out of my cheeks. Her grip was so tight,

I thought she'd surely dented my cheeks that day. I couldn't help but tear up.

"Don't you ever call me Grandma. You hear me, little girl?"
I couldn't keep back my tears, and as she let go with no remorse, as usual, the back door opened. I knew it was Momma Jean. I was saved once again. Full of hurt and pain, I bolted off toward Momma Jean. I didn't let her so much as step in the door before I buried my head against her thighs, hugging her tight around her legs.

The rage on Momma Jean's face was enough to set the Atlantic Ocean on fire. Her left eyebrow raised up, her jaws tightened, her nostrils flared with every breath, I'd never seen Momma that mad before. She kneeled to my level and whisked away my tears with her fingers and kissed my forehead and whispered in my ear as she hugged me tightly.

"It's okay, baby." Momma Jean's voice was ever-soothing, it could ease any pain. Then she stood and strode into the kitchen. Usually, Momma Jean commanded me to go to my room when these arguments erupted, but this time around, I trailed behind her.

"What is the meaning of this, Momma—I mean Lois." Momma Jean clapped her hand over her mouth after her slip of the tongue. Lois never turned around, but she continued to cook and hum. I knew Momma Jean was upset after I saw her put her hands on her waist and if her complexion was any lighter she would have been red in the face with furry…momma's chest danced rhythmically with every exhaled breath. She walked up to Lois and tugged her shoulder.

Lois spun around and pointed a steaming-hot wooden spoon, dripping red spaghetti sauce, an inch away from Momma. Even though Momma backed up quickly, Lois leaned into her and whisper-shouted at her. I couldn't make out what she was saying, but Momma stalked away, yelling, and Lois mumbled to herself like she always did.

Momma Jean grabbed my hand and pulled me out of the house. We went to our serene place, where we liked to go and hide out in such times—a little lake behind the church building. Whenever we went there, we always sat in the grass, and Momma talked to me as though I was an adult. She told me all her dreams and aspirations, and I listened because I knew she had no one else to talk to.

Our times at the lake were simple but priceless. My busy mom and I craved those times. The moment itself never lasted long, but the memory always stayed with me, even more so when Lois treated me meanly. Then I always took myself to my happy place with my Momma at the lake. Even now as an adult, I can't figure out what I did to Lois that made her hate me so much.

* * *

The second week of January 2014, St. Louis, Missouri.

"Brian!"

"Yes, Nandi."

I couldn't help but cry since I was having a horrible nightmare.

"What's wrong, honey?" Brian shook me fully awake. I couldn't talk. My tears had taken over my voice.

Brian reached for the nightstand on his side and turned on the light. I must have been fast asleep for a while because I did not remember falling asleep. The last thing I remembered was Brian handing me some Earl Gray and my over-the-counter sleeping pills. Everything after that was a mist until this horrible nightmare.

"I miss Momma so much. I want to go with you and the guys to clean out her house tomorrow."

He hesitated. "We already discussed this, and we agreed that it was best for you to stay home and rest."

I fell back asleep then, not a word of fight in me.

The next morning, I awoke to an empty bed and the sounds of the microwave chime and ceramic plates clinking together. Surely Brian wasn't in the kitchen making all that ruckus. He gave me no choice but to get out of bed. As I neared the kitchen, my nose told me he was making my favorite breakfast.

He stood at the stove, his back turned to me. I couldn't resist embracing him from behind. When we sat at the table with my favorite omelet and French toast, I had a refreshed love for my husband that morning. Every now and then, this happened to me, but other times I just didn't feel the love connection.

Momma loved him, but now that she was gone, would we stay married? She was the glue that kept Brian and me together. The old doubt came barreling back into my mind; did I marry him because Momma liked him or because I wanted to be married to him?

"Let's pray." Brian's definition of saying grace was a morning prayer that included everyone and everything but the food. Most times, when it came time to eat, the food was as cold as ice.

"Amen." After only a few seconds, Brian concluded the grace.

"Amen." Wow! He must have read my thoughts. Either that, or he was

in a hurry.

"I'll be over at your Momma's house all day, getting her stuff packed up so we can put the house on the market," Brian said as he multitasked the meal to his mouth.

What did he mean? "Put her house on the market?"

He laid down his fork. "We already went over all this with your mother and her attorney, remember?"

The agitation in his voice made me more uptight.

"I don't remember agreeing to that."

"Well if you hadn't been so..."

Brian caught himself and crammed more omelet into his mouth, probably because he knew the conversation would not go anywhere.

"If I hadn't been so what?"

For a man who didn't like confrontation, he sure had a way that could work my nerves.

"You know what." He shoved back his chair and threw his napkin onto his plate. On his way to the door, he kissed my forehead. "I'm heading over to Momma's house. I'll talk to you when I talk to you."

Once again, he did what he liked to do most: flee the confrontation. That was fine, but one of us had to be the adult. I'd have to carry on. My appetite was gone after he left. I gathered up all the plates and placed them in the sink. The inner me knew that without Momma, I might lose Brian. The stronger me tried to act macho as if I didn't care. I'd put on a show for Momma all these years. Now it was my turn to gain freedom.

* * *

Later, that evening.

I lost the concept of time. It felt like I had been sitting in my bathtub for a very long time. I knew it was night time because the sky looked starless and was silky dark through the small curtain–less window. I could feel my fingertips pruning as I sat in the now semi-luke-warm-freestanding oval tub; the tub that took Brian three months to install because he claimed he wanted a sentiment of the house he grew up in and being the cheapskate, he is he took on the project.

What's crazy is I can't remember the last time I took a long bubble bath but at this moment and time it was all I needed as I enjoyed my bottle of wine and thought of Momma. I purposely grabbed Momma's boom box before I soaked myself in the tub because I discovered the radio had Etta James CD Tell Mamma and all I wanted in that moment

was the first song of the Album on repeat. Etta James was Mommas Favorite Singer. I grew up listening to virtually all her records; when Momma wasn't listening to Gospel music.

Growing up, Momma over-extended her helping hand to help me overcome my "condition" as she labeled it, and all I did was look into Momma's eyes and give her false assurance that I was not a drunk like she so convincingly thought.

CHAPTER THREE

Next day...

This by far was one of the harshest winters I had experienced in St. Louis in a long time. Because of the snow, Brian had been working from home more than he liked. But no one could have predicted the forceful restrictions of Mother Nature. Would I ever get over Momma? I still called her cell phone just to hear her voice, and I would give anything to have one more day with her. Brian didn't know that I had not deactivated her cell phone yet. It was the only thing I had left of her—my voice of reason all thirty-nine years of my life. If I took that away, I would have no other physical connection to her.

"Here's your morning dose of herbal tea," Brian said as he entered the bedroom. I was glad to see he brought me some hot tea. He placed it on my nightstand and reminded me of my English college roommate, Patronella, who had introduced me to herbal tea. I, in turn, taught Brian so it could be to my advantage.

Brian sat on his side of the bed and kicked off his shoes.

"Looks like someone is trying to catch a nap on the job."

"That's easy when you're your own boss."

"True. How are the projects coming along?"

Sigh. "As best as they can." Brian's voice had a distressed tone.

"Honey, we need to hire some help for you. The business is growing

and you're working too much. The accountant already said we can afford to put at least two more architects on the payroll."

"Yes, but we haven't had time to put all the necessary information

together for hiring. Besides, I want to use that payroll money to get our personal financial situation under control before I start hiring people."

He paused, gazing into space. After several moments, I asked, "What's on your mind?" I knew my husband's face when he became focused in thought, as much as I have known him for twelve years I know that he would want to do anything in his power to save a penny....

He smiled. "I'm in awe of God. Do you remember when I started my business proposal?"

"I remember helping you draft it. I also remember all the people who

were against you trying to start your own business."

"And now those same people ask me for business advice." Brian paused while he shook his head and had a gazed look. "I'm glad I stepped out in faith."

"I am too."

"You know, if it wasn't for Momma Jean, I don't think I would have

been courageous enough to pursue my business. That Sunday night,

when I told her about my idea, her eyes lit up and she just

smiled. She said, 'You better go on, boy!'"

Brian laughed before continuing. "I still remember her high-fiving me,

then she went into a speech about entrepreneurship. She hyped

it up so good that when I left there that night, I couldn't stop

talking about it all the way home."

He scooted close to me. I couldn't remember the last time Brian and

I just sat around in bed, not thinking of the cares of the world. This moment was perfect and almost felt like my first few years of blissful marriage before the disturbances of life.

"I miss Momma." Brian whispered as he squeezed my hand.

"I miss her too. She loved you like her own."

"Yes, she did." Brian caressed my hand and sat in silence.

I took another sip of my drink. "This tea is extremely good. What did you do differently?"

"I used the secret ingredient."

"How do you feel this morning?"

I really didn't want to tell Brian that I felt like crap and I was terribly hungover because that would be inviting an argument that wouldn't turn out favorable. "Besides my head throbbing, I'm doing well. This tea is helping soothe me."

"Good. I thought maybe you would be hung over."

It's that condescending tone that dug deep into my last nerve. "Don't

start. It's too early in the morning for a lecture."

Brian sat straight up and faced me. "Why are you always on the fence?"

"I am not always on the fence."

It becomes so annoying when he tries to act like a board-certified psychologist and the advisor to all my life's problems.

"Yeah? I don't appreciate seeing my wife like that."

The shame washing over me was more than I could handle. I knew exactly what he meant, but I didn't know what to do other than to play dumb. "Like what?"

"Look, I'm not going there with you." Brian released his hand from the embrace and stood up.

"Good! Because I'm not in the mood." The last thing I wanted to hear was his cautionary tales.

"I'll be in the basement if you need me. We leave for service at five." Brian slid on his house shoes.

"That's too early."

"Besides dealing with all that snow on the highway, I also have to

unlock the doors, turn up the heat, and shovel the walks." He started for the door. "I expect you to be ready."

* * *

That quickly, he walked away from another confrontation. No one ever tells you the truth about marriage. Well, I take it back. Some divorced people have a lot of advice about marriage. There are books and classes and courses for married people, but at the end of the day, we should figure it out for ourselves. Then again, if someone had tried to teach me about the nitty-gritty of marriage, I would not have listened.

Brian came from a two-parent household, but I had known only one parent. I never had a father figure to look up to. Momma dated here and there, but I never really knew who the men were. Now that I'm grown, I understand that she kept them away until she felt secure enough in the relationship to introduce them to me.

I met only three of Momma's men. The first one was Phillip. He entered our lives right around the time we moved to East St. Louis from Mississippi. It wasn't hard for me to tell something was going on when Momma's days seemed longer than usual. They happened late at night and Momma's bedroom door would be closed. She usually left her door open, even if she was on the phone. I think she and Phillip dated for just a few months because it did not seem long before she was back to her normal routine. I never got the chance to know Phillip.

Mr. Kenny was my favorite among the three men in Momma's life. I was about twelve years old when Mr. Kenny came around. Of course, as with the other men, I most likely was introduced to him after he and Momma had established something solid.

Mr. Kenny was tall. He had broad shoulders and looked like a bodybuilder. He had a full but neat beard, which he occasionally stroked

when he talked. Mr. Kenny was not from the Midwest. I knew that because he had an accent unlike any I'd heard before.

When Mr. Kenny came into our lives, I thought he would be around for good. He used to pick me up from school. He made sure I did my homework and often helped me with it. If I wanted anything for school, he made sure I had it.

Mr. Kenny loved to talk. Sometimes when Momma had long days, he took me out to the local park on Fridays and talked to me about life. He was a smart man and viewed the world differently. It seemed as if everything in life was metaphorical to him, which went with his image. He seemed much older than Momma, but then again, grey hair doesn't always symbolize age.

Mr. Kenny's love for Momma was so overt that one could easily tell. Sadly, about the time I got used to him spoiling me and Momma, he disappeared from our lives. I don't know who was more heartbroken; Momma or me. His absence was profoundly felt because he was the closest I ever had to a father.

How could someone come into someone else's life and give them hope and happiness, only to disappear without any acknowledgment? After Mr. Kenny, Momma didn't date anyone, at least she never brought anyone around, until I was seventeen. Then she began seeing Dr. Larry Bentley. He was one of Momma's professors, from what I garnered. I shied away from getting to know him because the last time I got close to one of Momma's men, it turned out ugly, so the best thing to do was to keep distance.

He tried to form some kind of bond with me, but at that time, I was
consumed with my own boy-crush drama. Besides, he wouldn't stay around. The other two men had left us, so why give this professor a chance? It didn't help that he gave me a creepy vibe. He looked as if he had just stepped out of a 1970s hippy movie. I can never forget the tormenting smell of Brut. It was so strong, I could smell him a mile away. When I got home, I always knew if he had been in the house because of the lingering smell of his cologne.

His sense of humor was rather dry. I could clearly tell Momma was faking it when she laughed at his horrid jokes. Unlike the other two, he was short and scrawny-looking. He had a comb-over like no other. It always seemed as though he combed over three long strands of hair, and between those hair fibers, a silky and shiny scalp lay peeking through. His scalp was so shiny, you could almost read your future like a crystal ball. How could he be that much in denial about balding? His mustache
was always discolored as though he was trying to cover his grays.

I didn't understand what Momma saw in him. They seemed like opposites. But he stuck around through the rest of my high school and the first two years of college. One day, I came home in my junior year of college, and Dr. Bentley was history. Momma never spoke of him, so I didn't ask. I never had a relationship with the man, so I couldn't have cared less about his whereabouts.

* * *

That evening...

On any other occasion, I would have had an outfit in mind. But every time we went to Brian's church, I had to think hard and dig deep in my closet. He allowed me to be myself for the most part, but when it came to his church, he became somewhat of a fashion guru suddenly.

"Are you almost done, Nandi?" Brian hollered from the bottom of the staircase in the basement.

"Not quite."

I can't stand the feeling of being rushed...I knew what I was getting myself into when I gave that response. Within moments, he was going to pop into the bedroom, ready to go. Brian's thing was getting ready hours ahead of time.

"What's taking you so long?" he asked as he entered the bedroom.

"I'm finishing up."

He ogled my slightly low-cut dress. "Are you wearing that to church?" "I was planning on it."

Brian gave a sarcastic laugh. "I know you have something else to wear."

"Like what?"

"Didn't you see the dress I laid out on the chair?"

If Brian could have his way, he would have me dressing like a presidential first lady—not so like a Michelle Obama whose style I fancy but Brian would rather have me looking more like a back in the eighties presidential first lady that wore two-piece suits that looked to me like material from a curtain set.

"It's the midweek service. I don't feel comfortable getting too formal."

"It's not formal. Look at it." Brian lifted the dress.

"I don't get it. Why can't I wear what I want to wear?"

His jaw tensed as if he was having a lot of trouble keeping his cool.

"I'm giving the sermon tonight and would like my wife to look decent."

"You're insinuating that this dress is not decent?"

"That's not what I said."

"Momma bought this for me."

"Yeah, I know. Momma bought the dress for you when she was in Ghana, and you know what? I love it! But not for tonight. It's not even February yet."

Brian was in the mirror, tying his tie. I was out of words. The best thing for me was to maintain my silence code.

Brian could hardly keep a straight face. "Look, if you want to wear

your dashiki dress in the middle of January, you can."

"This is not a dashiki. It's a hand-made Ankara dress, and you know what? It's fine. I'll wear the dress you picked. And what do you mean it's not even February yet?"

Brian chuckled. "All I am saying is that dress is very festive." And he left it at that.

I knew exactly what he meant by "festive." He thought that because it's African, it should be displayed around black history month. I begged to differ. He knew how much I loved my hand-crafted tie-dyes and Ankara outfits, all thanks to Momma and her many travels back and forth to Africa. I felt they validated my mini FRO, and besides, they were fashionable.

Momma loved Africa. I was happy to see her living her dream of visiting different African countries and tribes. Something about her university studies and later profession made her yearn for a connection

with the motherland. She managed to travel to ten African countries and vowed that when she retired, she would move to her favorite one, which was Mauritius. She dreamed of owning a bungalow right by the beach, and she dreamed of rekindling her travels to the rest of the African countries.

"Are you ready, Nandi?" Brian asked as he walked out toward the hallway, tightening and straightening his Eldredge tie knot. Brian had this thing about his ties, suits, shoes, and shirts. When we were dating, he always made a point of drawing attention to his different tie knots.

It took me a while to catch on. He always asked me, "How's my tie? "And I, being oblivious to the factor, always said, "It looks good."

I wasn't paying attention to his intrinsic fashion–tie tastes, the way his socks color-coordinated with the trousers that had to coordinate with some color of the dress shirt. Then, to top it off, depending on the day, season, and occasion, he wore a tie or bow tie. If a tie, he tied different knots for different occasions. And let's not forget the cufflinks that must match some color of the whole ensemble.

I admit it puts a smile on my face every time I see him all dressed up and looking spiffy.

"I am in the car," Brian hollered from down the hallway.

I knew that was my cue. "Coming."

I couldn't remember what I did with my Bible, and I knew Brian didn't like me using my iPad to reference scriptures. I didn't get that, but it was grounds for a never-ending argument, so I had to make one more quick stop down the hallway. When I'd gone through Momma's belongings the other day, I had seen her nice-sized Bible.

* * *

The drive to church was always somewhat interesting. Brian liked to meditate while listening to his gospel music. I, on the other hand, was always consumed by week's plans, which, quite frankly, consisted of drinking. Everything else came after that. So very seldom did we hold any conversations in the car.

"I'll drop you off at the door," Brian suggested as usual, which made no difference as he had to unlock the doors anyway. After Brian parked the car he power walked to the doors of the church. "After you," Brian insisted as he unlocked the door and opened it. Then he rushed over to the alarm box and punched in his code.

"Have a seat in the sanctuary. I'll be outside putting salt on the walkway." He pulled his skullcap back on his head. The sanctuary always smelled like fresh pine. I'm not sure if it was the well-kept pine pews or air freshener. Whatever it was, it smelled different, a good different. Even though I shied away from organized religion, I couldn't help but marvel at church buildings, especially the earlier ones, built in the 1800s and early 1900s. It amazed me how much effort and care was placed into the finishing of these buildings.

This one was built in 1908. The church has since grown, so they have expanded, but they managed to keep most of the sanctuary preserved with the beauty of the stained glass that illuminated the sanctuary. Had this church been smaller, it would have reminded me of the little white brick church we attended back in Shuqualak, Mississippi.

"Sister Nandi Jean Wilkerson!" A familiar voice echoed through the
sanctuary and startled me.

"Reverend Doctor Bryden," I said when I caught my breath.

"What a pleasure to see you here with us today, young lady." The reverend drew in for a church hug, the one with the handshake between the torsos.

"Likewise, Reverend. I'm not so sure about the young lady part, though."

"Of course, you are! Anyone younger than I am is young." Reverend Bryden laughed.

"How have you been Reverend Doctor? I hope I am addressing you

correctly. I never know which title comes before the other."

"You can call me Rev. That will do it for me." His contagious laugh

engaged his whole body, his shoulders following the beat of the sound. The fact that he had more upper body than lower made it that much funnier. I liked the Rev. You could tell he was truly about ministry. Momma respected him as well, as she knew him from Mississippi.

Reverend Bryden had to be close to eighty-five years old, but he looked no more than seventy. Through the years, I have known him, he has always been as kind as he could be, sincere and loving. He and his wife took over the church about forty years ago, Mrs. Bryden is in a nursing home, the hardest choice he could have made. But her dementia was getting worse, and she'd been hard for the church-busy Reverend to take care of.

"Nandi, my door is always open if you ever want to come in and talk. I know the loss of a parent can be hard to come to terms with. Sometimes grief counseling can help you in that process." The reverend reached in his inner blazer pocket.

"Thank you, Rev. I'll take that into consideration."

"Here is my card and my direct office line. Please come in sometime to see me." Reverend Bryden handed me his card. Soon he became sidetracked by the entrance of the ushers. "Excuse me, Sister Wilkerson," Reverend whispered and started toward them. The inclement weather seemed to bring some folks to church earlier than usual.

"That's Deacon Wilkerson's wife." I could hear whispers coming from behind me.

"I think her name is Nancy or something like that. I know it starts

with an N."

I couldn't help turning around to see where those curious whispers were coming from. Then I decided to greet the two whisperers, who happened to be the mothers of the church as they have been two of the longest faithful members and the title mother is befitting to their ages. "Mother Jones and Mother Johnson, it's nice to see you two tonight."

"Oh, baby, I was just asking if that was you," Mother Jones said softly, while Mother Johnson nodded in agreement.

"Yes, it's me, mothers." Here we go. Let the judgment start to shine

brightly on their faces.

That's how I felt sometimes when talking to some of these mothers of the church. Oh, they'll sometimes be sweet enough not to say much to your face, but the looks give it all away. Mother Jones and Mother Johnson have been faithful members of the church from what Brian told me, they have been with the church for as long as the Reverend has been in the church, and they are the only two elderly people left hanging on to life as the rest of their generation had gone on to Glory and many the churchgoers now consist of the former generations adult children and their children.

"What you done child, cut your hair?" Mother Jones asked. She has never known how to use her inside voice, so whispering for her is like regular low talking to some other people.

"I cut my hair, so I can go natural."

"Natural?" Mother Johnson said in a condescending tone.

"It's the way to go nowadays."

I tried reassuring the old-school, old-fashioned, women-should-never-cut-their-hair committee that I was fine with my choice.

"She lost her Momma." Mother Jones thought she was whispering to Mother Johnson, but I could clearly hear them.

"Oh, honey. How have you been holding up?" Mother Johnson asked.

"The best I know how." Mother Johnson suffered a stroke back in the day that left her paralyzed in the arm and leg, which never slowed her down because she still got around well by herself with the help of a cane of course. She must be well in her late eighties, but her face always had a small smile and I know like Momma, if anyone else loved the Lord, it
was Mother Johnson.

"You keep that word close to your heart, you hear, Nancy?" Mother Jones said.

"Yes, ma'am." I reached in to kiss her on her cheek and gave her a hug. "But it's Nandi."

"Oh, baby! You know what I mean," Mother Jones insisted. I knew I would always be Nancy to her.

"Don't be no stranger to the house of the Lord, you hear?" Mother Jones hollered.

"Yes, ma'am."

And yes, the heads turned my way since Mother Jones was so loud. I had to take a few minutes in the bathroom before service started. Something about Mother Jones reminded me a little of Momma. Every time I thought I was making progress in my grieving process, I found myself in pitfalls of missing Momma. The church, the pews, and the mothers brought back memories of Momma and me going to church together.

* * *

The start of the service was what Momma lived for the most. She loved the praise and worship as much as she enjoyed the teaching. I couldn't but help hear a familiar song as I walked back to my seat. Every note of the songs reminded me of Momma. For a split second, it felt good to release my tears as the praise singers sang in their melodious voices.

CHAPTER FOUR

Twenty-eight years Earlier

I must say Momma did quite remarkably well in making sure I stayed within the church walls. She made sure it was a big part of my upbringing, and she made sure I would carry it into my adulthood. Before college, I was sheltered by and covered in religion. I never questioned why we went to church. I never questioned the church and its structure. All I knew was that if I sinned, I was going to hell. According to the preacher, hell was not a pleasant place. This always shot fear into me. My curious mind never ceased thinking of this "hell theory."

I used to wonder a lot about Adam and Eve. Were they in hell? After

all, they sinned first. Or was there pardon for them because they were the first humans on earth? Then I looked at the preacher man, preaching obnoxiously in the pulpit, and wondered deep down inside my naive mind how he kept from sin, and if that was even possible.

My curious mind took me on numerous guilt trips because I sometimes thought I was going to hell simply because I wondered if the "man of the cloth" was a sinner. I didn't dare ask Momma if the preacher man ever sinned. Those were grounds for banishment. But my curious mind was proven legitimately normal when I was sixteen years old.

All of a sudden, the once-thriving and growing church began to decline in membership. No one wanted to talk outwardly about the cause, but through the rumor mill also known as Bible study groups that Momma hosted at home, I heard chatter about the obnoxious and hell preaching preacher and his sinful ways. Apparently, he had impregnated a young lady in the congregation, and the fact that he had been married for over thirty years made the situation way worse than just another man's downfall.

The preacher's sermons always seemed to leave the small group divided. The same thing happened when the preacher fell into sin. The Bible study group bantered about the situation but didn't talk in depth. Some blamed the young lady for coming between the preacher and his wife. Momma blamed the devil. The rest blamed the preacher.

They always agreed to disagree and continued with the Bible study, no matter what issues were going on at the church Momma and I continued to attend. Even when we moved to St Louis, Missouri, we still attended that same home church in East St. Louis,

Illinois. Something about Momma and her loyalty to that church still baffled me up to this day, even after the "hell-preaching preacher" had been sent packing on his way with his loyal wife by his side.

Momma had worked hard to shield me from human flaws most of
my life, but she wasn't ready to explain to me the truth of man's flawed nature. Even in adulthood, when we ran into some old congregants, Momma lowered her voice when they started talking about the church, so I wouldn't hear their conversation. This confirmed to me that she was still trying to shield me from all human truths.

Little did she know that my pure eyes and ears were introduced to the cruel reality the day the preacher's affair ripped the church in half. It not only caused a drop-in membership, but it also broke a lot of hearts and ended a lot of friendships. Most of my friends, whom I had known since we moved to East St. Louis, were from this church.

Because of the differences in views, I could not hang out with or even see most of my friends. Sure, this preacher stomped the pulpit and embedded the fear of God in people, but his downfall only made me realize how human he was. If most adults had embraced him as a human, not a god, perhaps, there might not have been such a tear in the church.

As it was, Momma's way of talking was a loving kind of threatening. She always said, "Boys are not good for you. All they want to do is get you pregnant, and if that happens, then you and your baby are on your own." That was a scary thought for a thirteen-year-old, but it never stopped me from being boy-curious. Some of Momma's scare tactics drove me to curiosity. I knew she did the best she could as a single parent but wasn't enough to prevent me from my youthful mistakes.

I couldn't help looking at the boys in school and being in tune with the change that was overtaking my teen body. All of a sudden, playing with my dolls and riding bikes with my friends in the neighborhood stopped being fun. Instead, I wanted training bras, and I worried about how my hair and nails looked. My school days were filled with rotating boy-crushes. The only person I had to talk to about it was my best friend. Together, we claimed the same celebrity or school boy-crushes and lived for a day when we would say a simple "hi" to the boy as he walked down the hallway.

After school, when Momma wanted me to fill her in on my day's
activities, I always wanted to blurt out every detail about my confusing body changes and the boy-crushes. But I knew she'd merely tell me again what the boys are all about. She would encourage me to keep my head in the books. Then she would want to hold a prayer vigil complete with the holy oil. She'd anoint my forehead with it and then rebuke those boys away from me.

Besides, the last time Gary-Jon walked me home from school in innocence, Momma pulled up and asked me to get in the car. The ride home was tense. She lectured me about the kind of distraction boys are. Like a broken record, she always insisted, "all they want to do is get you pregnant." All I wanted was for my mother to act human for a second. I understood her concern, but she acted as though she was never thirteen

years old and never looked at a guy and thought he was cute.

* * *

Two months into 2014

Momma passed eight weeks ago, and I still had a hard time boxing up her belongings that were in my house. Not that I didn't want to, it simply felt so final. An empty room feels like pure life emptiness. Momma always used to say, "The best time on earth is the quality time people share with each other, doing nothing but the simplest of things."

This explained why Momma's downtime with me included little things like walking to the park, going to the free museum, doing arts and crafts, having simple picnics, and sometimes putting puzzles together. We didn't go on vacations like some, because during most of my earlier years, Momma was preoccupied with accomplishing her goals. So, she insisted that once she was done with school and landed her dream job,

we would gallivant the four corners of the world.

But by the time Momma settled in her dream job, she had other, greater plans. She wanted to settle in and make sure she knew all the ins and outs of her new career as the professor of African American Studies before we set sail. Once she became more and more comfortable in her career, I was in the later stages of high school and contemplating college. Every time she tried to plan a vacation, I was working or had plans with my friends for the summer.

My non-participation in Momma's trips never stopped her from enjoying her life and her career. In my teens and college, I did all I could to stay away from home, it seemed like, but never on purpose. Something about that freedom excited every bone in my body and made me feel like the free spirit I am. Momma's leniency was granted when I proved myself able to work and juggle good grades. Then she trusted me just an ounce more than she had before. In the midst of my crazy teen years, I managed to get a part-time job.

I had no idea what I was getting myself into, but I'd heard other kids
jabber on and on in class about their "cool" part-time jobs. Momma never talked about me getting a job, and I didn't talk to her about wanting one because I didn't take it seriously. But one day, I walked into our high school career center out of curiosity, after the "working-class students"
told me that the career center advertised jobs within the vicinity.

This was the first time I'd been in our career center. It was the end of my junior year. I had always seen the building and knew it was there, but I guess I wasn't curious about what they had to offer in my freshman and sophomore years. I thought it was a place frequented only by juniors and seniors since it was also known for its college resources.

The minute I opened the single door to the career center, I was greeted with warmth by Mrs. Bakenfoth. She was "the career center." This woman loved every part of her job, and you could tell it. She was soft-spoken and stood every bit to five feet tall. She must have weighed anywhere from 120 to 130 pounds, but I bet if she got on a scale, she would have been five pounds over her natural weight because of her 80s

"big hair" style. Her make-up favored her 1980s theme, and so did her fashion sense.

She guided me to the section of the building with job postings. At first glance, I found nothing that caught my interest. I decided that working wasn't my thing. As I started to leave, Mrs. Bakenfoth asked, "Did you find anything interesting?"

"Nothing." I knew I wasn't invested in finding a job I just came by to check it out and basically see what the hype was all about.

"That's too bad. What are you looking for?" Mrs. B. asked.

"Have you ever worked in a restaurant?"

"No."

"Well, you're in luck. I was getting ready to post this latest job at

the White Rabbit fine dining restaurant. They need food servers." She handed me a copy of the post. "Have you ever eaten there?"

Fine dining? Not a chance. "No, ma'am."

"Their food is to die for. It's a cute restaurant with a good reputation. You should give them a call." I could sense a warm glow expanding throughout her body as she spoke.

"Will do. Thank you, Mrs. B."

"Good luck," she hollered as I walked out of the career center.

I flung the paper into my backpack. This was the last week of school and the start of my summer, so my mind was mostly occupied with the adventures my friends and I would have in store for us.

That evening after dinner, Momma wanted to know my summer plans. I had forgotten about my career center visit. Momma sat grading her papers and talking to me about ways I could spend my time over the summer. "The new pastor and first lady would love as much help at church as they can get over the summer. Maybe you can give them a call and make yourself available to help them."

As soon as Momma suggested that I volunteer at the church, I remembered my career center visit as quickly as I had forgotten it. "Oh,
yeah! I was at the career center today. I think I'm going to look for a summer job."

I doubted myself, but Momma wasn't leaving any room for options here. If I didn't come up with something solid, I was going to be at the church all three months of my summer. "A job? Where is this job?" Momma raised her voice as she stopped what she was doing and looked at me with lines forming between her eyebrows. She stared dead at me, as if in doubt. Nothing against the new pastor and his wife, but if I left it up to Momma, she would have had me at the church 24/7 throughout the whole summer. I had to resort to something. "I'm going to apply at the White Rabbit fine dining restaurant."

She burst into a loud, obnoxious laugh, clapping her hands and stomping her feet at the same time. "The White Rabbit fine dining restaurant!" I was completely lost. I felt as though I missed the punch line, but that laugh was Momma's way of not taking me seriously. "Yes, that's the name."

Momma fanned herself with one of the papers she was grading. "I

know the name, child!"

"What's so funny about it?"

"It's not the name. The thought of you working is funny. But if that's what you want to do this summer, then I am all for it, as long as it's part-time and will leave you time to do some reading." Momma half shrugged and continued grading her papers. "Do you know it's a fancy restaurant?"

"Mrs. B from the career center told me that already."

"If they call you for an interview, you have to make sure you've dressed the part. This restaurant caters to the town's elite," Momma said, distracted in her grading process.

* * *

I knew Momma half-doubted I would get the job, so the next day, I made a special trip to the restaurant. In those days, you could walk in and fill out an application, unlike nowadays. I took Momma's advice and wore one of my church dresses.

Although this restaurant had a great reputation, it was smaller than I thought it would be. Its intimacy must have been what people sought. I was nervous because I had never filled out an application before. But I was drawn to the building's quaint exterior. From the outside, all I could see was a large patio with four tables and chairs, the tables set with coordinating linens. The inside of the restaurant was dim, and there was a fountain at the entrance. Every single table and booth had matching settings too, like the outside ones. A Doris Day record played softly in the background.

The manager greeted me, and after I finished filling out the application, he gave me a short but detailed interview. He said they would contact me with start dates and all the necessary information. I left there confident, and I should have been because when I got home I found a message from the manager. They wanted me to start as soon as possible. Oh, the memories.

After working there all summer and enjoying the environment, I

decided to continue with a part-time position when school started back up. The job was a catch twenty-two. Momma thought it would be just a

summer job, so of course, she was all for something that would occupy my time. I initially thought I would give this part-time working thing a three-month trial period until I started to get fond of the people.

That first job taught me a lot about customer service. I had to deal with grouchy people, unsatisfied people, downright mean people, weird

people, doctors, lawyers, judges, a few entitled celebrities, friendly people, and nice people too. At the end of the day, all I could do was smile and look them in the eyes. Mastering the "smiling and nodding" gesture wasn't easy because I had never dealt with these types of people before.

Once I made the decision to continue working throughout school, Momma became concerned because she thought my grades would go down. Because of that, I worked twice as hard to make sure they didn't. I saved all my little tips and paychecks. After six months of saving, I managed to get Momma the sewing machine she had always wanted. It appeared that was her latest reunited fond as she had always talked about her sewing days back in the day.

She told me how her great-grand mammy taught her different patterns on her sewing machine. Momma never talked much about her immediate family, but she talked a lot about her great-grand mammy. She told me how the old woman used to spoil her and how she learned

a lot of life lessons from her.

* * *

"What on earth is taking forever? You've been in here a long time."

"You caught me off guard. I'm sitting here reminiscing. I wanted to box up some of Momma's stuff, so we can take it to the church rummage sale."

"What's the progress?" Brian said with a small, delighted smile.

"None so far. I started to put the boxes together, then I started to think of Momma, and that made me think of my first job."

"Do you remember we have the meeting with the lawyers tonight?" Brian said with a look that told me he hadn't been able to keep the surprise off his face. "I'll be back to pick you up around six thirty."

I was anxious to get Brian going so he wouldn't stall and start an argument. I knew that brief pause and frown. He'd been deep in thought and, given the chance, he would have said something that would have led to an argument.

I never wanted to be one of those arguing couples, but each year, Brian and I seemed to do it more. We didn't want to, and usually, in the heat of the argument, Brian was the first to bail out. We became people who both thought our own opinions were better than the others.

Because of that, we stood our grounds, and it never went anywhere. Brian did so because he believed in the whole "head of the household" thing. I did it because I felt obligated to stand my ground. Either way, we had more lame arguments than crucial ones, if there is such a thing.

CHAPTER FIVE

Three months into 2014

The snow was still very profound and showed no sign of cooling off momentarily. It was as though the snow was on some chemical boost because it was quite strange for it to be as profound as it was in the middle of March. It made everyone wonder what the spring was going to be like. Patronella and I usually took some kind of road trip around the end of March or beginning of April. It's been a perdurable tradition of ours since the first spring break that we roomed together.

That year, she wasn't going home to England, and I was not going home, so we got all our saved money together and set sail for Kansas. It was a two-hour ride from Columbia, Missouri, where our college was. Kansas wasn't technically a spot for spring break, but it was where our money could take us. Besides, neither Patti nor I had ever been to Kansas.

Patti was from a well-to-do English family. Her father was a successful business mogul in England, her mother was a housewife, and Patti, the only child, had been raised in a home with two nannies and a gardener. I'd never heard of some of the elaborate after-school activities she talked about. I thought she was the epitome of the crème de la crème class, which was far from the way I was raised.

At first, I gave her the cold shoulder when she tried to get to know me. My own insecurities drove me to that. By the time I started college, my weight was 190 pounds, and I was only 5 feet 3 inches tall. I attribute my weight gain to the free meals from the restaurant where I worked or maybe the fact that I was never athletic in high school. Whatever the case, in a sense I was envious of her, and not necessarily of her background. She was unique, and not just her accent.

She was about 5 feet 2 inches tall and about 110 pounds, 25-inch waistline, thick, long, naturally kinky hair, nice toned body, and she wore a coat of the darkest, smoothest color I had ever seen. I couldn't get over her perfect nose and lips. Her nose was cute and small, her lips were full and yet even. A lot of people paid good money for facial features like the ones Patti had. If I had looked like her, I would have opted to model as a part-time gig.

She wore the biggest, whitest smile, which complemented her high cheekbones. Her British accent was fabulous, and she also spoke French fluently, as her parents were first-generation Haitian immigrants to England. After I got to know Patti, I saw her for the shy, humble introvert she was.

When Momma first met her, she was naturally drawn to her and considered Patti her other daughter. She loved to hear her British accent and loved the fact that she was wise for her age. I agreed with Momma— Patti always gave good, sound advice. She was a good example of responsibility, and that's how I knew she would go far in life. I had always considered her a great role model and figured the rest of her life would be great. Some people are destined to have a great life, and Patti was one of those people. I knew for a fact that, after college, she would soar like an eagle.

Eventually, she married Pierre, a Haitian-American born and raised in Chicago. His parents too were first-generation immigrants to America.

Patti and Pierre met in Chicago at a West Indies festival. Their wedding

was the greatest I had ever attended; a traditional Haitian wedding/ white wedding combination, and by golly, it felt like a royal wedding. Patti and her new husband decided to make Chicago their home. Their careers rose to great heights.

We decided to continue to take a few days off in the spring and drive to neighboring states for pampering, relaxation, and much-needed catching up. We didn't see each other much through the year and didn't spend much time on the phone.

* * *

I knew Momma half-doubted I would get the job, so the next day, I made a special trip to the restaurant. In those days, you could walk in and fill out an application, unlike nowadays. I took Momma's advice and wore one of my church dresses.

Although this restaurant had a great reputation, it was smaller than I thought it would be. Its intimacy must have been what people sought. I was nervous because I had never filled out an application before. But I was drawn to the building's quaint exterior. From the outside, all I could see was a large patio with four tables and chairs, the tables set with coordinating linens. The inside of the restaurant was dim, and there was a fountain at the entrance. Every single table and booth had matching settings too, like the outside ones. A Doris Day record played softly in the background.

The manager greeted me, and after I finished filling out the application, he gave me a short but detailed interview. He said they would contact me with start dates and all the necessary information. I left there confident, and I should have been because when I got home I found a message from the manager. They wanted me to start as soon as

possible. Oh, the memories.

* * *

Brian was finally gone to work and the first thing I wanted to do while laying on my chase was to open my bottle of Moscato. My cell phone rang. It was Patti. I'd never been so glad to hear her voice, and I gushed out my enthusiasm. "I was just thinking of our road trip this year and reminiscing about our first one."

"We've come a long way with this tradition." Patti laughed.

"What are you doing?"

"Having a glass of Moscato."

"At 11 a.m.? I thought you quit drinking."

"I've quit many times and failed at it. There. I've said it."

"Are you still attending your meetings?" Patti's concern was thick in her voice.

It's so annoying when people think they know what's best for you.

"Great. I hear it from Brian every day, and now you too."

"Hear what? I don't get it."

"Look, I don't want to go into it with you too about my drinking,

meetings, rehab..."

"It's your life and your marriage, and you're the one who asked me to help you stay sober..."

"Look, I appreciate your concern, but I will be fine."

The last thing I needed was someone castigating me about what I do for my relaxation.

"I'll call you tomorrow."

"Oh! Now you don't want to talk."

"Nandi! You've had more than a glass of Moscato. You are clearly

drunk, and I can't hold a civil conversation with you right now."

The phone beeped as Patti hung up.

* * *

I was nineteen years old and in college when I had my first alcoholic drink. Of course, it was underage drinking, but that's what we did on the

weekends when we wanted to be "cool" and hang with the big kids. College, for me, wasn't necessarily proving myself in the popularity circles like in high school. In my freshmen year in college, I felt the need to prove myself as "grown."

I don't know where that came from, but it was my mentality. I was away from home, I wasn't so sheltered and dictated to, so my freedom was my responsibility. I would never have thought I'd drink or put any mind-altering substances in my body, mainly because Momma did a great job at teaching me that my body was my temple. The simple fact that I was raised orthodox "holy-roller" Pentecostal, in which it's a sin to look at alcohol, let alone indulge in a lifestyle of impurity through substance abuse, kept me sober for a long time.

Believe it or not, some of those teachings saved me in high school. They shielded me from succumbing to my friend's marijuana smoking, drinking at house parties, and ditching school for their habits. I stayed focused then because I knew it wasn't my thing.

My tongue did taste an alcoholic beverage when I was sixteen years old at a house party. But I couldn't even swallow the drink. It tasted nasty, and I spat it out. I wondered how people could drink such nauseating drinks. I knew drinking would never be my thing, or so I thought. Even though Momma shoved Bible principles down my throat as scare tactics, I couldn't negate my natural, teenage curiosities. I felt as though curiosity was a teen embodiment.

Then, years later, I had this thing that has hurt my friends and burned

some bridges. Brian did his best to help me, placing me in three different private in-patient rehabilitation centers. He shipped me off to those undisclosed rehab centers so the folks at church wouldn't know about my supposed habit. He was in denial as much as I was.

I agreed to get help after my incident several years ago, Each time, I

came out determined, wanting to experience sobriety at its height. But all rehab seemed to do was give me a few months of sobriety. Then some life-altering deal sent me to the deep end and found myself back at square one. I've been to the meetings, I have had a sponsor and all the good stuff. Momma knew of my problem but, as with everything else throughout my life, she reacted by having no reaction. She would rather pretend the problem doesn't exist or insist that I need some kind of spiritual deep cleanses.

I started as a social drinker in college, far from my Christian upbringing. It aggravated when I found out that I didn't have to think or worry about anything when I was buzzing. After college, alcohol became my new "happy place." When Brian and I met, he had no idea how much I drank because I did so well at concealing my drinking habit. He fell in love with the sober Nandi, who was visible and clean during the day.

* * *

Brian and I had been trying to get pregnant for a couple of years, and it eventually happened. Her name was intended to be Brianna Jean Wilkerson...I will always wonder why it happened that way. For years and months, I thought God knew I would be an inadequate parent.

As usual, Momma couldn't give me any emotional support. Her classic no-reaction-as-the-reaction was now a part and parcel of Momma.

Every now and then, she threw in her casual phrase: "Pray about it." I wanted to tell her it felt as though God didn't hear my prayers. He seemed distant from me in the neediest time of my life.

Brian's solution was therapy, but I couldn't stomach another therapy, another Christian counselor, another psychological evaluation that left me wondering about my mental state. It all seemed too overwhelming, too much for me to handle.

* * *

"Nandi! I'm home." Brian's heavy footsteps pounded the hallway
toward the kitchen. He flung open the master bedroom door, stalked into the room, and shook my shoulder quite roughly. "What are you doing in bed at three o'clock in the afternoon? I told you we had an appointment with the attorney."

"I thought the meeting was this evening."

"I specifically told you it was after work." Brian reached for the empty wine glass on the nightstand, brought it to his nose and, no doubt, I knew he smelled the alcohol. "What am I eating for dinner?"

I was enjoying the soft comfort of my pillows as I was propped up against them in a sitting position watching TV. "There are mashed potatoes and salmon in the fridge." I didn't have an ounce of energy to move.

"From last night?" Brian's voice rose to a ten on his volume box. Usually, I would have gathered myself before Brian got home so I can freshen up, cook and play the bountiful position of wife but at some point, everything changed. Brian started coming home at unpredictable times,
which didn't give me enough time to clean-up my act.

"Ladies and gentlemen…this is what I am working hard for?" Brian said biting his jaws and clapping his hands. "The house looks like a mess it hasn't been cleaned in a very long time…and now I can't even get a decent meal. This is just great Nandi!" Brian huffed as he threw his hands in the air.

"What's that supposed to mean?"

Brian paced from the door to the bed and back. "You know exactly what it means. Our finances are upside down because I've been paying for all your treatments and extra counseling that our insurance won't pay for. I'm out there all day, busting my butt, to come home to a drunken wife and scraps from last night's dinner!"

"So, you've come home on your high horse?" I had to prop myself up for this conversation.

"High horse?" Brian's anger distilled down to a bitter laugh. "Does any of this mean anything to you?"

"Of course, it does."

"Then why don't you act like it?" He slammed his fist on the chest.

"What do you want me to do?"

"I want you to act like you care about life, I want you to act like you care about us, and I want you to care about your body instead of that junk you keep filling it with." He paused in his tirade and glared at me, all compassion gone. "Why are you crying?"

"I...I..." I couldn't find the words.

"What, Nandi? I'm listening."

"I want to quit. I'm trying."

"Trying what?" Brian's tone sharpened.

"I don't know. I need some time to think through life or something." It's all overwhelming. For the last several years, my life has been a big blur. *I want it to change.*

Positioned by the window with his body turned towards me Brian said.

"How is it different this time?"

I wish I had the magic answer for him, I wish I could tell him what he wants to hear, and it would come true but I couldn't...

"what do you mean?"

"Every time you relapse, you promise to change. You promise to do better and you're always sorry. How is your sorry any different this time than it was the last time?"

"I know I've fed you with empty promises. They weren't empty on purpose. I want to quit. I hate what is going on with me, and

I would give anything to be normal and sober." I couldn't hold back my tears of shame.

"Then why won't you quit?" His sharp tone hadn't eased off a bit.

I wish he would quit nagging. "I am trying. I don't know why I can't

quit."

"I want to help you, more than you will ever know, but my help toward your recovery has cost too much in more ways than one. You're not getting any better, and we can't keep spending so much money on something that's not working."

"I'm trying."

Brian shrugged his shoulders. "Well, your trying is not good enough."

"I get it. You want me to stop, to turn off the switch, and suddenly be an exemplary wife. Right?"

"Don't turn this around on me and act like I don't understand. At first, I didn't. But after all those meetings for family members of addicts, I know that you can't just stop. I've been more than willing to work with

you through this process, but we're not getting anywhere." He raised his voice again and pulled his phone from his pocket. "This is causing a lot of stress and pain for me."

Like I wished this in my life. "I never wanted to be an addict...

I... I want different out of life right now."

"Do you really?" Brian asked, scrolling on his phone.

"I do."

I was scared to fully admit that I wanted help because a part of me felt I wouldn't succeed. I have tried rehab, counseling, and outpatient and still relapsed.

"Okay. For starters, you can figure out how we're going to pay this $50,000 to the mortgage company without losing our home. Then you can find a way to pay off the outstanding balances from the rehabilitation centers."

"If this is your way of reminding me and feeding my guilt trip about

the funds I misused, then it's working. I get it. I was supposed to oversee all the mortgage payments and bill payments, but I failed us both on that and used it for myself and to feed my addiction."

Brian paced the room. "My intention is not to do anything indirectly. I want you to understand the enormity of this situation." He tucked his phone into his side pant pocket and folded his arms across his chest.

"I get it."

"Just get ready so we can go and hear what the lawyer has to say." "Whether you believe me or not; I truly am sorry."

"If you are, then I suggest you hang out with the ladies at church more. Maybe then you can start to rebuild your relationship with Christ." Brian's voice lowered as he sat down beside me. "I have no doubt that you can beat this. I know you can be restored and overcome this monster, but you need to believe it as well."

Somehow, my conscience awakened at his kindness. As always, he was

faithful to his duty to me.

* * *

Something about Jerry's office gave me the heebie-jeebies. His little one-room office was nestled in a multi-purpose leasing plaza that catered to all kinds of random businesses. When I say, "all" kinds of businesses, I mean they had a shrimp and fish shack, an alterations store, a beauty supply store, a nail spa, a uniform store, a knock-off clothing store, and other little, bitty obscure offices.

"So, I have the paperwork all prepared for you to sign." Jerry said as he slid the paperwork across his desk towards Brian.

"Nandi!"

Jerry caught me off guard as I tried to peak a read on what Brian was

signing. "Yes, sir!"

"How are you holding up?"

That question made me feel a little emotion stirring up because I knew that deep down inside, Jerry was genuine and then I knew that he was really asking because he was Mommas close friend and he missed her too. "I am doing ok, thank you for asking."

Jerry Nolan's law office was the only professional office in the whole plaza. My best guess was that he picked a budget-friendly office but not necessarily a client-friendly one. He had been a penny-pincher from the time I met him. Mr. Jerry, as we knew him back in East St. Louis, retired from the circuit court as a notable judge. Now he dedicated his later years of life to numerous pro bono cases. In my heart of hearts, I knew he could afford a better location if he wanted it.

After Brian signed the paperwork he gave it back to Jerry and Jerry walked out of the room, Brian and I were in silence, I, on the other hand, wondering why he needed my presence if he was the only one signing paperwork, Jerry returned about five minutes later with a folder and handed it to Brian.

"Here are your copies." Jerry said as he handed Brian the folder. "Do you have any questions for me?" Jerry asked while smiling generously.

"No. Not now." Brian said as he stood up.

I took that as my cue to get up as well.

"Nandi! I am so glad you came with Brian." Jerry said as he shook my hand.

"Thank-you Jerry, it's nice to see you too."

Brian shook Jerry's hand. "Thanks again judge for all of your help."

Jerry opened the door and escorted us out to the hallway. "You two stay blessed."

"You as well judge." Brian said.

Judge Nolan never married and never had any kids. Like Momma,

he spent most of his years traveling the globe. Also, like Momma, he graduated with a law degree later in life before transitioning to the bench as a judge.

I've known Judge Nolan since I was young. He was good friends with Momma, and he too lived in East St. Louis at one point in time. Momma met him at church and as two adult scholars, they immediately clicked. I tried to break the awkward silence in the car ride home.

"So…was that all the paperwork for Momma's house and stuff?"

Brian Nodded. "Yeah…some of it." "What do you mean?"

"It means just that, Nandi." Brian said in an agitated tone.

"Ok! Excuse me for aski…"

Brian interrupted. "I am sorry babe…just got a lot on my mind and

would rather talk about all of this when we get home.

Mr. Jerry had aged gracefully over the years. He was seventy-five years old but looked only sixty-five. He still bowled with his league and he still traveled the world. When I was younger, I secretly wished Momma and Mr. Jerry would eventually get married. Or should I say I wished he would be my father?

He was a prime example of a life turned around. Mr. Jerry knew no stranger, as Momma would say. Every chance he got, he gave his testimony, the one in which God delivered him from his worldly lifestyle. Every time he spoke of the events leading to his deliverance, he teared up and his voice cracked as he spoke. I'd never known a grown man

with such passion for God.

Whether he was out to lunch, dinner, or just hanging out, Mr. Jerry always stopped what he was doing and tapped into whatever stranger he zoomed into, flagging them down and talking about God. He was a bold Christian but not aggressive. I liked his approach better than the hell-preaching preacher I grew up on. Mr. Jerry's soft voice made him seem that much more compassionate and less intimidating. He had a way of bringing the best out of people, acted as a messenger from God sent to earth to save all of humanity.

I wondered why Brian wasn't pulling into the garage.

"I have to run to the office real quick and get all this paperwork stuff

together." Brian said.

"It's late, you should do all that paperwork tomorrow..."

"Look! I don't have tomorrow to do this it has to be taken care of as

soon as possible, I will be right back."

"Ok, whatever!" I got out of the car as fast as I can feeling annoyed.

Mr. Jerry started his auto-detailing shop at age eighteen, using drug

money as capital. He'd been a big-time dope dealer and held down a large portion of Illinois and Missouri back in the days. He nearly met his maker a couple times. Most of the people who ran with him were either killed by rivals or incarcerated.

He started selling drugs when he was twelve years old. He didn't know any better. The streets raised him when his mother was strung out on crack, and he never knew his father. Mr. Jerry talked about the hungry days at home and how he, the oldest child, had to do what he thought he had to do to make a quick buck and feed all five of them. None of the siblings knew their fathers, but they all knew their mother was an addict, too engrossed in her own addiction to raise them.

She spent most of her time away from home, binging. Until age eighteen, she bounced from foster family to foster family, never knowing her biological parents. Then she resorted to working in adult entertainment, and to cope with her life's circumstances, she experimented with crack, the drug that eventually took a great hold of her. Her poor choices led to a string of unhealthy relationships with men who kept leaving her after she became pregnant.

One of Mr. Jerry's proudest foundations is the one he pioneered to

help young mothers and women find themselves. Every time Mr. Jerry talked to me about his mother or his upbringing, I felt terribly sorry for him. He would have given anything to have a mother-son bond. I always knew he told me about his mother, so I would not make the same bad choices in my teen years.

CHAPTER SIX

Easter 2014, St. Louis, Missouri

"**N**andi!" Brian's stern voice awakened me as he stormed into the bedroom, holding the phone. "We're leaving for service at 9:30, and you have a call." I turned over in bed to see him holding out the cordless phone. "Who is it?" I mouthed. He covered the mouthpiece with his hand. "It's Patti." "Tell her I'm sleeping," I whispered. She never calls this early especially on a Sunday.

Brian laid the headset on the table and walked off toward the door. "Here you go."

I answered but I didn't want to talk to Patti.

"Happy Easter!" Patti said, giggling.

If I wasn't fully awake, then I was now, thanks to the hollering over the phone. "Happy Easter to you and yours. To what do I owe the pleasure?"

"That's no way to address your best friend."

She was right. I had to slowly sit up and give her my full focus without any caffeine yet in me.

"Why are you so chipper this early in the morning?"

"He rose today!" Patti said with throaty laughter.

He rose every Easter If I remember correctly so what's really going on? "You are never this excited about Easter."

Patti murmured. "Okay, you got me, but seriously, I'm excited..."

I had to shift some more pillows on my back for extra comfort to prepare myself for Patti's news. "Excited about what? The anticipation is killing me."

"I'll give you some of the scenarios, but before I start, I want you to

know that Brian is okay with everything."

"Don't play games with me at six in the morning. What's going on?"

Patti Laughed. "I've planned our yearly road trip for the first week

of May, and we're going to take as long as we need. I'm paying for the whole trip, and Brian has agreed that you should go." Patti stopped talking to catch her breath.

This sounded fishy. "Are you and Brian planning on dropping me off at some rehab somewhere?"

"The world doesn't revolve around your condition, Nandi." Patti said.

If I know anything about Patti is the simple fact that she is a person that does things with a solid reason behind it for the most part...she has

never paid my half on our past trips. "What's the catch?"

Patti Sighed. "Do you want to go?"

I would most likely be excited if I knew a little bit more about where we're trying to go or where Patti wants me to go. "Where are we going?"

Patti's voice lowered. "I can't tell you which states we are going to—"

Something felt amiss...I have known Patti for a long time and she just doesn't do things to do them without a reason. "Why not?"

"You're my best friend, so I'll let you in on a little information. I've

been putting together an experimental group."

I knew it! Why am I not surprised? "I'm to be a guinea pig?"

"Not exactly. For my final Ph.D. project, I decided to conduct a yearlong group experiment. So far, this has helped eight out of the ten. The last time I spoke to you, it dawned on me that I might be able to help you figure this all out..."

"Figure what out?"

"I want to use my background and this experiment to give you some

answers to the lingering questions you have often talked to me about."

"So, what are you now, a psychologist? And what makes you think

you're remotely competent to help me?"

"Look, I might not be able to fix you because I am not God. But this

is way more than you're doing. You need help!" Patti's annoyance rang in her voice.

Now if she told me that she had had some kind of addiction in the past, maybe I would take her seriously. I couldn't help but doubt her competence especially when I knew her whole life has been like a never-ending peach cobbler with each bite as imaginably sweet.

"I see what you're trying to do, and I appreciate it. I'll get back to you later tonight after Easter dinner. This is a lot of information to process, and the fact that you wouldn't tell me where we're going makes me pretty much leerier."

"Okay, because I am a total stranger?"

"Don't be sarcastic."

"You have my number. Call me when you're ready to grow up and take some responsibility." Patti's tone sharpened, then she hung up.

* * *

May 2014

I remember bits and pieces of that horrible Easter night. I remember being upset at Brian and opening a bottle of Moscato. After a couple of glasses and a few bites of my tiramisu, everything became a blur. I knew I was in an ambulance because the sirens were louder than I had heard before. Then a man asked several questions and I could hear him talking medical jargon with another man. His voice was what I remembered most of that ride: "Ma'am! Ma'am! How much have you had to drink?"

Then he yelled at someone else. "She's non-responsive. Call the ER and tell them it's probably alcohol poisoning. The patient is in an alcohol induced coma." Coma?

I could hear him loud and clear but, for some reason, I couldn't talk or open my eyes. After fighting inwardly, I blacked out, only to awaken to bright fluorescent lights and strangers in white lab coats, hovering around me.

"Nandi!" a female barked at me.

I still couldn't make my mouth move. I was secretly hoping I was

dreaming.

"Nandi! Squeeze my hands."

By now, I couldn't move any part of my body.

Then I heard a machine going berserk. I felt myself convulsing while the same female voice yelled out for a doctor. Shortly afterward, I blacked out.

* * *

"Rise and shine, sunshine."

I looked towards the unfamiliar voice and struggled to open my eyes. It felt as though I was an awakening for the first time in my life.

Out of confusion, I asked. "What am I doing here?"

The stranger's voice sternly spoke. "Honey, you were brought in two

weeks ago, with alcohol poisoning."

"What do you mean?"

My body was in so much pain, it felt like a punching bag.

The voice of the stranger drew colder. "Your husband found you lying unconscious, face-down in your vomit."

* * *

Patti took the liberty of staying with me in the hospital for as long as

I no longer have to be spoon fed, and to my surprise, she never judged or reprimanded me for getting myself into what apparently seemed like self-destruction. Patti was downright receptive. I began to feel like I could confide in her without the fear of being attacked with the biblical implications of my actions.

"What do you think about dreams?" I asked.

"Do you want my educated take on dreams or my spiritual belief?"

"How about a spiritual take? That psychological stuff throws me off."

"What did you dream of?" Patti continued to gaze out the window. "What are you looking at?" I wanted to make sure I had all of Patti's

attention.

"I'm just people-watching. This is a view to die for." Patti giggled. "Go on with the dream."

The only person I could freely talk to about my dreams without feeling judged in any way was Momma. Patti came from a background that believed in dream translation. She'd on more than one occasion mentioned to me about her mother's ability to interpret dreams. "Please don't call me crazy." I said calmly.

"I think I've known you long enough to know that you are far from crazy and I certainly hope you don't hesitate to tell me anything because of how you think I might view it. You are my best friend and you should trust me with whatever information you want to tell me, ok!

"Ok…it's just that…"

Patti walked towards my bed as she spoke. "Just that what Nandi?"

"Never mind."

Truth is, I couldn't bring myself to telling her how the dream went because I feared she might think I was only being delusional. In the dream, I was running down a cobblestone road, yelling, "I will die for Jesus." The road was empty and narrow; kind of like ancient Rome from the movies. Then I looked back over my shoulder and saw two men in black clothing. Even their heads and faces were covered, so all I could see was their eyes.

I was down on my knees with my arms up in surrender, and I continued to yell, "I will die for Jesus." My eyes were shut tight and I couldn't stop myself from saying it. I said it over and over and over, even though those two men had guns drawn on my back. Finally, I heard a clunking noise. I turned around and they had thrown the guns on the ground and were running the opposite way. Shortly afterward, I awoke, and they said I had just come out of a coma. I ended up telling Patti just a little portion of the dream because I wasn't ready to hear what she would say.

"Wow." Patti sat down at the foot of the bed. "I'm speechless."

"At first, I tried to ignore it, but the more I ignored it, the more it kept coming to my mind. But I don't know what it means." Honestly, I wasn't sure I was ready to find out the meaning of the dream.

"Okay, you got me there. It's amazing though." Patti scooted close to the bed, grabbed my hand, and cleared her throat. "I really need you to go with me on this road trip."

"I don't know..." I said depressingly.

"I'm the only one left, other than your husband, who tries to protect

your feelings and can tell you the truth," Patti said in a lowered voice.

A sense of dread came over me. "What do you mean?"

"Your husband has been moving stuff out of the house."

"What stuff?"

"Furniture, clothes, dishes, you name it. Everything and anything that belongs to y'all."

"I don't get it." I am afraid to fail at sobriety again. This is the hardest thing I have ever had to face, I know what it's doing to me, to Brian to us as a married couple but I am deathly terrified of failing. What else is there if rehabs and counseling sessions didn't work for me before?

"Nandi, the bank has foreclosed on your home. I didn't want to be the one to tell you. But you should consider coming on this road trip. You need time to air out, get the feel of a different environment. Besides, I want to help you overcome this beast." Patti squeezed my hand and smiled.

Foreclosed? "How is a road trip going to help me?"

"Do you trust me?" Patti spoke softly with a crackling voice.

"It's all my fault, I misused our money and I misused Brain's trust... I don't know."

"Say yes to the road trip, Nandi." Patti's eyes filled with tears.

"Patti, don't do this to me. You know I don't want to go." My heart is torn. I am afraid I won't succeed.

"How long will it take you to realize you have a problem?" Little did she know that I had more than one problem in my hands.

"I am not in the mood for this kind of talk." I said blatantly. It felt so annoying to hear people castigate me over and over.

"Well, you're in no position to hang up on me or walk away, so you are going to hear it all." Patti reached into her purse and pulled out a tissue, but I wasn't sure who it was for, her or me.

"I need time to think it through." "I gave you time two weeks ago, look where you ended up." Patti's voice turned harsh. "You and your husband are one paycheck away from being homeless, and Brian is stressing. You can't afford any more medical bills."

My anger shot to the top of my head. "Are you saying this is all my

fault?"

"Well, Nandi, you're the one in the hospital bed." Patti's voice held

as much agitation as her eyes did. "We're leaving on Memorial Day

weekend. Brian has a suitcase packed for you."

"Wait, what?" Things were moving way too fast for me.

"That's right. I'll be by your new place Friday morning before Memorial Day."

"So, you had this all planned, and yet you still wanted to hear my take?"

Patti smiled. "I was just giving you time to get used to the idea. It's going to happen, one way or the other."

CHAPTER SEVEN

Road trip 2014

The most important thing for me as a friend in this road trip was to show Nandi how much I truly supported her and wanted the best for her because I almost feel as though she might have had doubts in my motives, and I know through my degree that, trust is an issue among addicts.

"Are those raindrops on the windshield? There goes my day!" Nandi exclaimed.

"Don't get all depressed on me now." It's a good thing we are in the car throughout this summer storm.

Sigh. "I know this is random, but what was it like, growing up with a father in your life?" Nandi asked.

Her sigh matched my own. "I don't know what to tell you because I don't have anything to compare my life to. Besides, he was gone half the time, so I often didn't feel like I even had a father." I tried to cover that blanket statement of hurt with my nervous laugh but who was I fooling?

"I'm a bit shocked at that."

Nandi was on to me. "Since we are in the truth-mobile, being honest with each other on this road trip, I admit that yes, that's the way I feel about my father." I paused for breath. "People think I grew up with the ultimate lifestyle, but I didn't. Now that I am older and wiser, I know that most of those things were a front. My parents put on a great show, acting as though we were living it large. Don't get me wrong, my dad was and is a wealthy man. But he invested minimal time in his family."

"Why do you think he stayed away so much?" Nandi was fidgeting with her hands.

Talking about myself and upbringing has never been an easy one for me. He had another family out there. At first, he spent the weekdays with us, but things changed momentarily; then we got only his weekends. Before Mom told me about his other woman and kids, I was oblivious of his absences because Mom always enrolled me in extra-curricular activities after school. I thought Dad was traveling on business.

I had no idea of my mom's pain. Now that I'm married, I can only imagine it. When I found out about my father's other family, I was in my last year of high school. I'd planned to attend Oxford University, but the news was so devastating, I wanted to leave England altogether. I never wanted to go back. My emotions took me on a wild roller coaster ride. I had looked up to this man my whole life, and now he had the nerve to abandon my mother and me in such a manner?

The thought of it all over again brings my heartbeat to a palpitation, a palpitation of the fear of being abandoned by a man I looked up to and l loved. I can't help but not to shake the feeling of my own husband walking away. After I forgave my father, it took me many years to meet his other family. It was easy to forgive my father but physically hard to forgive the circumstances. For the longest time, I walked around angry at my father's other family. But after I met them, I realized it wasn't their fault. I had wasted years, being angry at them because my father missed the most significant parts of my life. But he had lied to the other woman as well.

She had no idea that my father was married and had a child. My forgiveness process was complete when I met my father's other family. Before then, I walked around in bitterness, anger, and resentment. That was one of the reasons I stopped going to church when I started college. It had nothing to do with God but everything to do with my dad.

"Long story short my dad had another family out there." I couldn't tell her my hearts pain due to fear of old feelings surfacing. "See! I didn't grow up in a perfect family unit like you thought."

"Oh. My. Gosh. Patti…I am so sorry to hear that. I had no idea."

"It's OK. It's the thing of the past I don't like dwelling on too much."

By reassuring her that I was over that part of my life I was assuring my own heart. I had to blow my nose before I could continue. "Even as a grown woman, I find it hard to embrace what happened and what is. I have taught on biblical forgiveness and embracing and loving those who hurt you, but for some reason, it's easier to teach it than to experience it."

"I'm sorry Patti. I am just trying to process this all in."

"No need to be sorry, it's the story of my life." I kind of understand my life today because in a sense I feel as though my dad's decisions taught me a lot about life and God. Forgiveness is so powerful that the lack of it can cause things to happen to us later in life. For instance, I was so broken that everything that happened to me during college seemed to be a direct reflection of my anger, bitterness, and resentment.

"I feel so bad that happened to you. But forgiveness, huh! What do I know? I'm just an alcoholic." Nandi said begrudgingly.

"That's not true." I said to assure her.

Nandi gazed out the window as though in deep thought. "If it's not true, then what is?"

I had to think real hard for an honest and yet not so complicated response. "You're not the only person in America who's bound by something. Some people are bound to money, some are bound to caffeine, some to food or other substances. Anything can enslave you if it takes a higher priority in your life than God does."

Nandi glanced over at me and cleared her throat and softly said. "What about you? What are you bound to? Or have you ever been bound to anything?"

I could hear the doubt in her voice as she asked the question and in my mind, I felt as though she might have perceived me as a perfect human because every now and then she knew how to throw in the 'Miss Perfect' sarcasm notation to our varied conversations.

Truth be told, I don't know if I was ready to indulge her with the "for-real" me. What would she think? After all these years, she has viewed me in a certain light now to throw in me from my past would almost feel as though I've been dishonest all these years, even though we have never tried to know each other in-depth before this moment. "Oh, no, missy. This is not about me." I wiggled in my seat a bit-trying to avoid her question.

Nandi agitatedly spoke. "Well, then, we might want to establish some more rules and regulations."

"The ones we have in place are fine." I quickly insisted.

Nandi narrowed her eyes at me. "I get it. It's all about the alcohol,

right?"

"It's not that. It's just that I'm not sure if I'm comfortable sharing this with you yet. Don't get me wrong, I can tell you anything, but..."

"Then tell me!" Nandi paused to catch a breath. "I get it. You want to know all about me and, yet you don't want me to know about you. If we're best friends as you say, this doesn't make sense." "Okay, fine," I said.

If there was one thing I knew about Nandi, it was the fact that her temper was like a bullet in the gun chamber ready and willing to dislodge at any moment. The reason why I don't like talking about it freely is that the first few years of my marriage were rough on me. I didn't think Pierre and I were going to make it until my co-worker invited us to her church.

We eventually went because I could feel myself dropping into a deeper slumber than I had when we first got married. "I connected with the pastor's wife, and you know how hard it is for me to trust people. The purging of my soul started months after First Lady Loretta started working with me."

"Purging?"

"Yes, like you, I battled a stronghold, this thing that kept me bound to sin. No matter how much I hated it, the other person, and myself, I still did it. I prayed for it to go away. I thought I was going to be this way for life."

Nandi's mouth was wide opened as her voice became louder.

"Wait! Your marriage was in disarray?"

"Oh, honey. Disarray is not even the word. I know the hand of God

saved my marriage."

"What was this thing that bound you?"

I never thought that day would come, a day I would open up to someone about what I wasn't particularly proud of. I could feel my palms sweating and my stomach knotting up. "I'm trusting you with my deepest secret." I drew a deep breath, my knuckles white as I gripped the steering wheel.

"At one point I was a sex addict." I said it so fast hoping she didn't hear me. And at first, I really thought she didn't hear me because she did not say anything back, that minute felt like an hour.

"Are you pulling my legs?" Nandi looked at me with disbelief. I exhaled softly as though a weight had been lifted off my shoulders. "I am dead serious." I exclaimed.

Nandi was shaking her head from side to side slowly. "I am having a hard time believing you." She said with a crackling voice. "I mean I am sad for you, I really am but…I just can't wrap my mind around it. I mean you are so perfect to me." Nandi raised her left index finger and wiped the single lone tear.

I had a feeling she was going to take this a little rough. "You don't believe women can be sex addicts?" I said with a light smile to lighten her up.

"I don't believe you could be a sex addict. I am sorry I am getting all emotional it's just that I would have never guessed for a day in my life that you had a struggle in life."

I didn't know for sure if Nandi was hurt at the fact that her perception of me all these years had just been dismantled or I wasn't sure if she was emotional because she felt a connection to my pain as an addict.

"Well, I was." I rest assured her without a doubt in my voice.

My father's brother, who lived in Haiti, visited us most summers. At first, when it happened, I didn't think much of it. I was confused, thinking it was normal until it started to happen frequently. He used to have me sit on his lap. Then we played all kinds of secret games. As I got older, the games changed. When I was about thirteen, a sex abuse counselor came to our school to talk to us about normal and abnormal behavior. Then I knew something was wrong.

I couldn't believe I had been so blindsided by the truth. The games, the weird touching, the weird look on his face, the awkwardness, the secrets, they should have been enough to give it all away.

After that, I repressed the events that had taken place between the ages of nine and twelve. Then I started to repress all my memories. My dad's brother did something illegal in England and was banned from returning when I was twelve. I should have been happy about that, but I wasn't. By the time I was fifteen, my body started feeling all kinds of ways I could not describe. It was the deception of yearning to be touched. By the time I was sixteen, I was fully sexually active.

The boys could do nothing to satisfy me, so in a sense, I never knew why I did it. I never liked the boys. I was embarrassed to talk about it, as all my friends were virgins. I lost interest in church and church activities because I felt as though God had allowed my uncle to violate me and leave me vulnerable. By the time I moved to America for college, the addiction had completely taken over, and I was at my wit's end. I was so embarrassed and ashamed that I would have traded places with a prostitute because they got paid.

"Patti, why didn't you tell me you were going through this in college? I could've tried to help you." Nandi said in a concerned tone.

"If it makes you feel better, I couldn't discuss it with anyone...I was too ashamed and afraid of being judged..." I wiped my free-flowing tears with the back of my right hand and struggled to talk through my tears.

"I worried about the pain it would cause my parents and friends if they knew or, worse yet, what if I contracted an incurable sexually transmitted disease? Then I met Pierre and I thought he would help me. But I was terribly wrong. The bondage put my marriage in jeopardy."

The truth of the matter was, Pierre wasn't enough for me and my needs. The last thing I wanted to do was hurt this man who genuinely loved me, so I fell into a deep depression. We tried marriage counseling and marriage workshops, but they didn't work. Finally. "We began attending the church my co-worker invited us to, and the pastor's wife there spoke life to me."

"Oh, the one you invited me to back in the day?" Nandi said as she cracked her window open. "Exactly! You have a good memory."

My eyes started to open to the truth. I realized my addiction had escalated when I came to America. By then, I was so angry at my dad for not being there for Mom and me. I grew much angrier and more bitter

when I found out he wasn't there because of this other family.

"Its fine now Nandi." I said hoping to dismiss this tense conversation. I thought that if he had never been with this other family he'd created, then I would never have been sexually abused by his own brother. If dad had been around, I'd have still been that innocent virgin I needed to be, and I wouldn't be tussling with my flesh's desires. I was bitter about the bits and pieces of a horrible memory that played in my mind like a sporadic movie preview whenever it chose.

"You know what, Patti?" Nandi softly said as she adjusted her seat to an upright position. "What a familiar place...for so long I wondered if I was weird or abnormal to want to wash out my memories and thoughts of my life, but here, you have it my own very best friend had the same exact feelings...I don't know whether to be happy or sad, happy that I am not weird but sad because you went through a lot."

"I know it's like information overload. I thank you for listening." I spoke while admiring the green crops that decorated the acres of land. Back in the day before I knew how to forgive my father, my anger would turn to hate, and I went for periods without talking to my father. The more I resented my father, the angrier I became. My emotions were like an out of control Shanghai Maglev. And when I got married, nothing changed within me.

Most times, I was tempted to feed into my addictions, fighting my thoughts and raw emotions. At times, I found myself on chat lines, flirting online with other men while I was married. "I gotta confess something to you, Patti." Nandi took in a deep breath and released. "I don't know how you survived it all to live to tell me. Looking at you I would have never imagined that life once took you down the old-dark alley."

"Girl, all I have to say is by the grace of God! Because after First Lady Loretta started working with me, I started to feel slow changes. She stuck to me like white on rice, and I tell you, she has a sense of being led by the Spirit."

I took a swig of my water and cleared my throat as I continued to talk. "The enemy had managed to blind me in deception, but only when I confronted the pain, hurts, and anger of my past could I transition into a healthy relationship with God." Reality is, the transformation didn't happen overnight.

It took a couple of years and even now, I am still growing in the Lord. But I can tell you that I am nowhere near where I used to be. I was born again and delivered from sex addiction.

"I hope you don't think I am trying to sound facetious or anything like that but…do you think or feel like you are totally normal again?" Nandi mulled around the question.

"You know what Nandi? Today, I can enjoy my husband the way God created me to as Pierre's wife." Gosh, that was a sentiment that was worth framing.

"Now, in my job, I specialize in addiction because, like Lady Loretta, I want to pour into someone else's life. That is why I can relate to you and what you are going through, and that is why I want to help you as much as I can. You see, I am not perfect, after all."

CHAPTER EIGHT

Road Trip 2014

The last time I traveled down on highway 55 was when Momma and I left Mississippi, and the only reason I remember was that I couldn't pronounce the town Sikeston. "When you were battling your addiction, were you afraid to die?" I had to ask Patti the nagging question in my mind.

"There was never a day I didn't think about it. It scared me to know that if I kept it up, I might die in my own fleshly desires. The scary part about addictions is knowing that you don't want to live that way anymore, but can't stop doing what you hate," Patti said boldly.

"I know you and Brian care about me, and I'm sorry for being apprehensive about this trip. But the truth is that I don't know how I ended up in this predicament."

"Oh, hon. It is part and parcel of the trials and tribulations of life. But from now on, we must go forth and not dwell on why it happened," Patti said as she exited highway 55.

"Where are you going?"

"To get gas and something to eat."

Patti pulled the car over at the gas station in Sikeston, Missouri, and headed in the store. When she returned to the car to pump the gas, I couldn't help wailing over my life. It was painful in the moment to face my problems and situation in a sober mind frame…I was really craving some wine.

Patti opened the passenger door. "Oh, Nandi…"
Sniffling through tears, I accepted the tissues Patti pulled from her purse. I hated for Patti to see me that way. "I'm tired of it all.
Patti murmured encouragement while rubbing my back.

"Why me? Why did I have to go through this?" I literally feel like the universe is against me."

"It's okay. I'm here to help you, and we're going to get through this." Patti shut the passenger side door, pumped her gas, and then positioned herself back in the driver's seat. "Are you hungry?"

"No." I didn't have an appetite to eat. I wanted some wine, some liquor, something with an alcohol percentage in it.

"Nandi!" Patti hollered.

"Huh? What?" Patti's voice startled me.

"Oh, my goodness. Are you okay?" Patti's right hand was on her chest to the left side as though she was clenching her heart and trying to stop it from coming out of her torso.

"I'm fine, why?"

"You were in such a deep daze, I thought you were getting ready to jump out of the moving car," Patti said, looking as if she was trying to fight back laughter.

I shook my head left to right and trying to figure out how long I had

been dazed. "I was in deep thought, that's all." I tried to play it off.

"Do you care to share?"

I pointed out the window. "Look at the pretty dairy cows. Do you ever wonder why only the black and white cows are dairy cows? I mean after all, don't all cows have udders?"

"Stop switching topics." Patti said with a smirk.

If I told her the truth about my incident eight years ago, she might confirm that I have a problem and, frankly speaking, I didn't feel like hearing her mouth about it. We'd been on the road for close to three hours, and yet it felt like an eternity. Then again, I'd always confided in her. Maybe I didn't want to tell her because I was ashamed of what I did, but if she found out later, she'd be even more disappointed in me. Maybe I should stall our conversation...

"Have you spoken to Pierre?"

Patti laughed. "Nice move, but I know what you're trying to do. No, I haven't spoken to my hubby. Now can you be the open book you said you were going to be? It's not fair, I just told you my biggest secret, now your turn?"

That moment, I felt like I couldn't hold back anymore because she trusted me more than enough to tell me her secret. "I never said I wanted to be an open book. I did say I didn't care to be your guinea pig."

Patti muttered. "Be a good sport then and play the guinea pig."

Ugh. If she wanted to know that bad, I would have to tell her.

"Remember my accident eight years ago?" I reluctantly asked secretly hoping she wouldn't remember.

"The one that messed up your tendons and stopped you from practicing medicine."

At that moment, I knew it was going to be awkward. She remembered precisely. "Do you remember my best friends from high school?"

Patti coiled her mouth to the side and shouted. "Andrea and Clara." "Yes—well…"

I guess it was when crazy Clara came down for my thirty-first birthday. At that time, Brian knew I drank casually. He has never been a fan of any drinking, as it's against his religious beliefs. For the first four or five years, I thought I was doing a good job covering my trail. Well, except one incident earlier in our marriage, right after we buried Brianna.

He found a few empty bottles of wine in an isolated corner I had kept them and got really mad at me. I managed to convince him they were helping with the grieving process, and he bought into it. From that day on, I became more cautious of what I did with the empty bottles.

Brian worked long, hard hours, trying to establish his architectural business. By the time he came home most nights, I was passed out drunk. I had a good regiment going on, so no one can fault Brian for not knowing sooner. I always managed to take a shower and then douse myself with perfume. I brushed my teeth, gargled with mouthwash, and went to bed with a cough drop in my mouth. I was methodic and calculated up until my accident.

That weekend, Brian wasn't comfortable with me hanging out with Clara. Brian and Clara never really got along because Brian thought she was a con-artist. I hadn't seen Clara in years, ever since she moved to Atlanta. So, I thought it would be an awesome time to meet up with her. Momma Jean was never fond of Clara or Andrea. She was always skeptical about those two, but who was I to say differently? They were my best friends, and in my teen years, I thought Momma Jean didn't know anything about my friends. Clara came to the house to pick me up in her rental car.

I could tell she had reached her limit of drinks, so I drove us to the restaurant, my favorite sushi place in Maryland Heights. We sat there and talked for hours. We talked about everything, we ate one sushi roll after the other, we drank sake wine, we laughed, we giggled. For a while, we forgot we were grown-ups, so much so that the next act didn't seem like a very grown-up decision.

Since Clara had been drinking longer than I had, I offered to take her to her hotel room where her husband was. It was the stupidest thing for me to do. After I dropped her off, instead of calling Brian, I figured I'd drive myself home. After that, all I remember is waking up in the hospital. I knew I was in deep trouble. It felt like a bad nightmare. I just wanted to go home but I couldn't.

Brian later told me that I hit a median on the highway and the cops had to take a chemical blood test from me since they found empty bottles of alcohol in the car. I tried explaining to Brian that they were not mine. And they were not. I knew better than to drink and drive in the car. I never before that day would have thought of driving drunk. But apparently, my blood alcohol level was triple the legal limit and I was facing DUI charges. I would never drive with open containers of alcohol. I'm a medical doctor or was one. But it's taken me this long to understand how much I messed up my life. Brian was disappointed and hurt, our home was cold tension for the next two years while Brian paid the court fees, lawyers' fees, and all the other fees associated with the accident.

Momma, she was Momma. But I knew she was disappointed in me. I wish I could take back that day, that night. I wish I had listened to Momma and Brian. I was in and out of court, I was given three years' probation, my driver's license was revoked. I had a record and there went my license to practice medicine. I went from being a new, young MD to nothing overnight.

Two years earlier, I lost all I looked forward to, so what was left of me? I couldn't practice medicine, so all those years of school and money went down the drain. I get that I placed myself in that predicament, but sometimes it's too much to handle. I'm still surprised Brian hung around after all. He won't forever.

"Yes well, what happened Nandi?" Patti insisted.

"Huh, what?"

"You paused after you asked me if I remembered your friends Andrea and Clara…it's as if you were in oblivion or something. You were just gazing out the window mouthing off and I thought you were gathering your thoughts till five minutes later you didn't say anything!" Patti giggled.

"Oh, I'm sorry. Never mind…I don't really feel like talking about it

right now."

Patti shrugged her shoulders. "It's cool…I am here for you, Nandi. We are going to get through this together," Patti said softly. "It wasn't easy telling you what I had to tell you, so I respect it if you need time."

* * *

By now, we had just entered the great state of Arkansas.

"When are you going to tell me where we're going?" In my mind, I had a few guesses, but I knew Arkansas wouldn't be one of the correct guesses. I just couldn't see Patti taking me to Arkansas. Though I must say, Arkansas is a hidden beauty. Years ago, Brian and I visited Branson Missouri and we decided to go through Arkansas as a tour. We ended up in Bentonville Arkansas the home of "Wally world" or Walmart as it is known. The ride in Arkansas was absolutely breathtaking. And yes! I would do it again.

"I know how much you love surprises," Patti said sarcastically.

"You know I hate them... I was just thinking, when did it hit home that you had a problem; I mean did you have a rock-bottom?"

"I hit rock bottom after I'd been fighting it for a while. Poor Pierre was clueless. Early in my marriage, I used a lot different online chat rooms."

"Like on-line chat rooms?" Not what I was expecting to hear so I immediately stopped playing candy-crush on my phone and listened in.

Patti continued to talk cautiously.

"Yes. I had been chatting with a fellow named Dean, purely flirtation. He fed into my sex addiction. The more we chatted, the more I felt my flesh burning up, as though my urges were on the verge of an outburst."

"So, there was an urge you couldn't control in other words?" By this time my phone was in the cup holder and I had repositioned my body to face Patti mainly in a surprise of what she was saying.

Patti gave out a nervous laugh. "I had been trying to self-restrict myself, but

without the power of the Holy Spirit in me, I eventually caved. One day, Dean decided we should meet up at a local hotel, and I agreed."

That was something I would have never imagined Patti being capable of. "You were not scared?"

"Well… I feared getting caught by Pierre. Now, mind you, Dean had been offering to pay for the event in the hotel room, and I repeatedly told him I wasn't going to take it. I was not going to become a prostitute." Patti was rubbing her right palm on her jeans all the while trying to multitask the air vents as she continued to talk.

"Addiction is cruel. Now that I think about it, I was determined to meet up with Dean. There I was, a married woman, and I didn't even think about how my husband would feel or what it would do to my marriage." Patti said with remorse.

"I am Shocked-Patti! Not shocked in a bad way, but shocked that you were actually in that predicament." I don't think a person that's not an addict can begin to fully understand how one thing can be so bad for you but you want it anyways, despite the consequences.

"It gets worse." Patti said as she paused to sigh. "My flesh wanted what it wanted, when it wanted it, and that's why it's so dangerous to be held captive by your flesh."

I know that storyline way too much. "Unbelievable…." I was speechless.

In a sense, I kind of understood then, why Patti was passionate about helping me. Only if she knew I wasn't against her help but more so afraid of my own willpower. In a sense, I was afraid of failing again.

Patti was gripping the steering wheel tightly with both hands at the 12 o'clock position if the steering wheel had a voice box it would definitely tell her that she was choking it. "After I agreed to meet Dean, I arrived at this rinky-dink motel in the middle of nowhere. I texted Dean and he texted me with the room number. I walked up to the door, and right before I knocked, something told me to walk away and go home; not to do what I was doing. Patti stopped talking and shook her head. "This time I repressed that inner voice. I felt as though I was burning so I went ahead and knocked."

"Oh my gosh." My eyes widened as I gasped for air. It felt like a very intense move.

Patti's voice sounded somber. "Just the thought of it all makes me sick to my stomach, now that God has opened my eyes to the truth. I think about all kinds of potential scenarios that didn't matter while I was bound."

"It does sound scary." I said.

"What if he was a serial killer? What if more than one man had been in that room that day? My goodness! I thank God for saving my life."

"Honestly that could've been the case but I am glad it wasn't." I couldn't but hear what she'd been through. It almost sounded unrealistic to me.

Patti sighed before continuing to talk. "Anyway, Dean opened the door, looking as dashing as he had in his on-line pictures. My pulse raced, but I thought it was because I was nervous. I walked in, and when Dean closed the door behind me, two men with police badges came out of the bathroom and arrested me for solicitation of sex."

Like momma, I always wondered if people feel a tangible God or is it more so like a warm and fuzzy feeling on the inside when they "feel convicted." "What exactly did you feel? You mention God a lot but I know I don't if I have that kind of relationship with Him."

Patti grew a big smile; the kind of smile folks draw up after you ask them to talk about their children. "Funny you ask Nandi. I didn't think I had a relationship with God either at that time but telling you of my story today as a person with a relationship with God I know it was God then." Patti's big smile persisted while continuing to talk. "I never thought I was better than anyone else, but I knew jail wasn't for me. My life was both sad and happy as I fought a monster no one else could understand. How could I have had such lack of control over this stronghold?"

All of a sudden, the clouds in the sky seemed to become darker and darker as though we were driving into a fierce wall of the

Nimbostratus clouds in which I really didn't care for in that moment. All I knew to look out for during these summer storms was Emerald green clouds and or funnel clouds; Momma always said those where the Tornado clouds.

CHAPTER NINE

Road Trip 2014

The further away from St Louis, we got the more I wanted to be back home. It's one thing anticipating a road trip knowing where you are going and it's another thing being on a road trip and not knowing where you are headed.

"What is your deepest, darkest secret?" Patti asked.

If I blurted out Brianna to her then I know she would have a follow-up question that my emotions are not even ready to think off and let alone speak of.

"I'd have to think about that. What about you?" I tried to digress.

"I can't say I don't have any, but I don't want to talk about them today." Patti tried hard to contain her laughter. "But you want to ask me about my secrets?" We simultaneously burst out into laughter.

"Tell me something Patti…how is your relationship with your father

lately?"

Patti gripped the steering wheel a little tighter before speaking. "It could be better. It's not that I don't love him. I do." Patti paused and sighed before continuing. "I don't know if he will ever change. Not a day goes by that I don't pray for him to change his lifestyle. My poor mother still hangs in there, strong as ever. I used to think they stayed together because of me, but when I went away to college and they continued their marriage situation, I knew my mother loves my father. What's crazy is that I often ask God why He is taking forever to answer my prayers for my dad."

"Miss Holy and Sanctified is losing faith?"

"I didn't say that. It's natural to have questions." Patti said defensively.

I have often wondered what devout Christians do or if they do anything when they feel like their prayers are not being answered.

"What if he doesn't change?"

"He will. Even though I have a million and one questions about him, I know God will turn him around."

Patti always reminded me of Momma's faith. Momma just knew

without a doubt, nothing could sway her any other way in her belief.

"This is random, when are you and Pierre going to multiply in the

family?"

Patti cackled with laughter as though I'd said a joke. "Whenever God decides to bless us. I'm psyched about being a mother for my husband's children. Every now and then, I think of what their names will be and how we will raise them."

"'Them, as in multiple children?" "A few dozen." Patti laughed.

"What are you all trying to do? Start a reality show?"

Patti shrugged her shoulders. "We might! But seriously, we wouldn't mind three or four children, because Pierre and I know how it feels to grow up wishing for siblings."

"I did too."

"That's right. You too. What about you and Bri..." Patti caught herself and looked at me with remorse. "I'm sorry. I wasn't thinking."

"It's okay." I thought people would have forgotten about the miscarriage, but apparently not. It used to bother me before until Brian helped me understand people mean no harm or mockery by asking such a question. The car was momentarily filled with an awkward silence.

"Wow, look at the sunflower, blossoming in the wild." Patti's obvious attempt at changing the subject made the tense situation even worse. "It's fine. It's just that..." I don't even know where to begin even if I was to begin to tell her.

Patti's tone grew concerned. "What is it? Talk to me."

"Well, as you said, it's natural to have questions for God. For the

longest time, I questioned God about my miscarriage."

"I would have had the same questions if it had been me," Patti said

with compassion.

"Did I do something wrong, something that made me undeserving of a child?" I had to crack the window a bit to get fresh air and clear my mind of the memory of pregnancy.

"Brian truly loves you. You have a good husband."

It's not what I wanted to hear at that moment, but she had a point. "I know he does, and I don't know how he can be so patient with me. Some wives are not sleeping right now because they don't know where their husbands are or who they're with." My chest felt full of emotion just by realizing in my sober mind how good my husband was.

He tried his best to help me through the miscarriage ordeal, but his words couldn't cement to my internal pain. Every now and then, I felt her feet pressing against my belly button. All I ever dreamed of was being a mother. It's funny how life happens. Sixteen weeks into my pregnancy, I was the happiest woman alive.

Then, in the blink of an eye, my happiness turned to sorrow. I knew

that morning when I awoke that something didn't feel right. It was a strong gut feeling like no other, but I went into denial. I minded my business all day until Brian got home late that afternoon. The craziest thing was that the baby was drawn to her father's touch. From the moment I first felt her little kick, she responded to Brian's hand on my belly as if she knew he was her father; they had a connection.

When Brian got home and talked to Brianna and rubbed my stomach

as he always did, I tried to convince myself that she was just tired. Or maybe she was mad at Daddy since he had been away on a business trip the last couple of days. He asked if she'd been kicking that day. Then the stone-cold, gut-wrenching truth hit me in the face. I hesitated to answer because I wasn't sure if her inactivity was my imagination or if I was losing it.

I remember shaking my head, and the next thing I knew, he grabbed his keys, my purse, and our insurance cards. Then he grabbed me. He didn't even give me time to change from my maternity pajamas. In the car, I started to feel faint. I rubbed my belly profusely and talked to Brianna, telling her everything was okay, that we loved her, that we would take care of her.

When I walked into the emergency room and the nurses came out with a gurney and whisked me off to the back, I knew. No one was saying anything to me. I demanded answers and all I kept hearing was, "we need you to relax." How can anybody relax while someone's sticking big IV needles in their arm? One nurse was pumping up a blood pressure cuff on my arm, and then someone dashed into the room with a portable ultrasound machine. All he said was that he was doing a routine ultrasound. Brian paced in the background. When the sonographer was done, he packed up his machine and headed for the door, speaking not a word to me. But Brian wouldn't let him out.

He went back and forth with him. The sonographer insisted he couldn't release results, but he did assure Brian that our physician would come in to talk to us soon. I could hear my husband praying under his breath. Then I started to feel faint and weak, and I blacked out. When I woke up, Brian was by my side. I felt as though something was wrong. I rubbed my belly and...

"Patti, please pull over." I couldn't get my door open quick enough. I had to prop my feet out on the ground to connect with the earth as I breathed in some fresh air. Reliving my memory, I felt sick because I could smell the hospital's odor when the doctor dished me out a cold plate of sorrow. The thought made my stomach drop, my pulse race, and my hands sweat. My throat tightened as though I was in a chokehold, fighting for breath.

"Nandi, are you okay?" Patti grabbed an empty fast-food bag from the backseat. "You're hyperventilating. Breathe in and out of the bag."

I could feel my chest heaving, I could hear Patti's voice, but I couldn't speak. My airway seemed constricted. I could feel the soft wind from the speeding vehicles on the highway, and my heart felt as though it was getting ready to jump out of my chest.

"Father, I pray you touch Nandi right now, in the name of Jesus. Give her strength to fight through this. Touch her mind and her heart, and let her say yes to You, God. Please give her total salvation and deliverance from this bond. Free her mind from past hurts..."

"Patti! You can let go of me now."

"You scared the living daylights out of me. One minute, you were

sitting at the edge of the seat with your feet outside touching the ground, and the next minute you started to hyperventilate and slide down." Patti helped me stand up. "I pulled over in a dangerous spot. Let's go and grab a bite at the next restaurant we see. Do you need help getting in?" Patti said while holding the car door open.

Feeling weak and nauseated I could barely speak. "No, but food sounds good. I'm getting hungry."

All my energy had been sucked right out of me. I knew I had a hard time thinking about Brianna, but I had no idea it would hit me that hard.

* * *

Twenty-Three Years Earlier

Steve and I had survived hanging out with each other for some time. I couldn't tell you that I was in love because love was an unfamiliar language for me. I liked talking to Steve but I can't say I was all in at that time. Rather, I kept it going because Clara and Andrea kept it going with their boyfriends. I didn't know what a boyfriend was. I kept Steve within proximity just to say I had a boyfriend. I didn't want to be the only one at lunch not talking about a boyfriend, so Steve was a good prop.

The hardest thing was keeping Steve a secret from Momma. I'm surprised we went undetected all those months. Lord knows how many times I wanted to tell Momma about Steve. But every time she talked about one of her friend's daughters talking to boys, she said the girl was fast. Momma did not believe in dating. She believed young people should court and then get married. And courting should always happen after people got settled in their careers.

Before I met Clara and Andrea, I thought that was the Christian way
and that it would get me to heaven. Small wonder that I thought I was abnormal for having feelings for the opposite sex.

I never thought I would keep secrets from Momma or lie to her. And every Sunday, our pulpit-stomping, hell-preaching preacher reminded us that we would burn in hell because of the lies of our mouths. But he had told the biggest lie of all times. It was a shock to me to learn at age sixteen that his cloth was not so holy after all. Would he be exempt from
the burning process of hell? Surely not.
It had been a year since the malicious scandal broke loose in our church and ripped the congregation apart. I was still trying to comprehend the reality of the truth. Unlike some, I thought the preacher was being framed. But Momma and I ran into him at the mall with his very pregnant current wife, also known as his former mistress. It was an awkward moment. Momma Jean gave me some change and told me to go to the candy machines.

Little did she know that the candy machines were within my line of sight. I inquisitively watched their conversation. I knew my Momma's gestures when she was mad, and all I could see were hands flying all over the place and head bobbing. How I wished I was a fly on Momma's collar so I could hear the conversation. It abruptly ended when the former hell-preaching preacher grabbed his now-wife's hand and stalked away from Momma.

Momma turned around as though looking for me, so I averted my face and acted as though I was window shopping. The ride home was the quietest ride I'd had in a long time.

Momma didn't speak all the way home, that was a first. When we got home from the mall, she went to her room, and all I could hear

was her praying. She hollered at the top of her lungs and wailed in prayer. I tiptoed toward her door and pressed my ear to it because I was concerned. I had heard Momma before, hollering in prayer, but this seemed different. I couldn't make out all the words through her cries, so I went back to my room to finally mind my own business.

After the prayer, Momma seemed normal again. She made dinner and we talked. I often wondered what the truth was behind the scandal. Sure, I'd come face to face with the truth in the mall, but I wondered if some of the rumors swirling among the saints were true. If anyone had the latest news, it would be the church folk. The paparazzi had nothing on the saints.

Supposedly, after the hell-preaching preacher impregnated the young church member, the board voted him out of his position. I heard that was not why the church split in half like a tattered piece of fabric. The split occurred because the hell-preaching preacher was going to divorce his wife of over thirty years and was going to marry the impregnated young church member. The board and all voting members wanted the preacher to stay married to his wife and end the affair. When he refused, the church was left with no option but to remove him from his position.

Half of the church members stayed, and the other half left, hurt and disappointed. Momma and I stayed because Momma had sentimental attachment issues. We'd joined the church at its start, and she had invested her talents in raising up some of its ministries. She had built a great reputation and had bonded with the pastor, his wife, and their family. The church was the only family Momma and I had; because of that, she was determined not to leave but insisted that the devil had gotten ahold of the preacher.

Everybody there was in emotional turmoil because he had founded
the church. Most of the members were charter members like Momma. As for me, the effects of his action included the loss of great friendships. That hurt me because, at such a young age, I was in a battle I never signed up for. This left me in a deep quandary of faith. If a preacher can stumble, then what about a person like me?

Other than that, my eyes were wide open. The church I thought was so perfect was flawed and filled with imperfection. This led me to wonder if the rest of our beliefs, such as courting after establishing oneself in a career, were also perfect imperfection filled with untrue realities. I wondered if the adults just made that up to discourage what would follow if teens dated early. Then temptation would be imminent and things such as pregnancies and all other supposed sins would be on the horizon.

Would it have been better for Momma to tell me to wait to court until I was older so I would not fall short? Or was career-courting a true Christian mandate? After the church split, I had all kinds of questions. Either way, I was being awakened to more realities. The perfect and pristine world Momma had worked so hard to maintain in my mind was crumbling down, and no one could reshape it. Not Momma, not the hell-preaching preacher, and certainly not me. Momma didn't want me to realize this yet, but the church was flawed, its people were flawed, the preacher was flawed, and guess what? I must have been flawed too. Talk about a rude awakening.

Our church was never the same after they voted the hell-preaching
preacher out of his position. He married the impregnated woman and he resigned from preaching. I didn't even know a preacher could do that until I heard the rumor mill speaking of it. I always thought that once a preacher, you will always be a preacher. But his abdication from the title surely meant he was done.

I wondered if he felt guilty for what he did. Then I realized that remorse was as far from his heart as the east is to the west. He proved that himself by not apologizing to the congregation.

The church tried a few preachers, but you could still feel the thick
cloud of tension within the church. After the hell-preaching preacher packed and left without a trace, we could all feel the competition among the remaining church members who prided themselves as candidates. These church-members-turned-candidates felt they were called to lead the church. This stirred the whirlpool of tension deeper while we waited for a full-time preacher.

Those who acted as interim pastors found themselves in battle with those who wanted the position full-time. By the time the church hired their first permanent pastor, the tension was so thick among the members that you could cut it with a pair of scissors. It was strongest among the leaders who held interim positions and the new pastor. Those ferocious interim wanna-be-full-time-preachers of the church managed to chase away the new pastor before the ink dried on his contract. After that, several more came.

The longevity declined with each hired pastor, which led me to question the position even further. Even if I was grown and lived per God's highest standards and held all possible credentials for the position, I wouldn't have wanted it on a silver platter.

But who was I to say? I think the members of the church were so hurt that, rather than letting another stranger into their pain, they wanted to try to fix the hurt by promoting one of their own.

I never heard Momma talk about the drama at the church. Rather,

during all the drama and position ego, Momma was more isolated. She stopped hosting Bible studies at home. Instead, she read more of her Bible by herself, and I saw her in prayer more than ever. Amazingly, the hell-preaching preacher's former wife continued to attend the church with her family.

The church later merged with one of the local megachurches in town

as a solution to the leadership issues. It was awkward at first, attending such a big church, but Momma and I adjusted better than some of the remaining members. With this transition, our old church lost yet another batch of members, because they wanted to remain a small and quaint church.

Momma thought it was a healthy merger because the church was struggling financially, barely keeping the doors open after the first loss of membership. She said that if the church continued without solid leadership, more members would leave, which could cause the church to close for good.

Steve was my current voice of sanity during the madness of church and school. The church drama was no excuse for my behavior, but it was the cause of my way of thinking. Sometimes, when Momma had to work late, I let Steve pick me up, knowing very well that I was never to have company at the house or leave home after I got in from school.

But all care was now on the side bench. This was Nandi's time. Even with that, all Steve and I did was ride around the neighborhood. Sometimes we went to the park and walked and talked about life. Other days we grabbed some food from the cheapest fast-food chain in the neighborhood and just sat in the parking lot to eat and talk without a care in the world. Then I headed home, threw on clean pajamas, and acted as though I had been home the whole day.

Before that time in my life, I absolutely, positively couldn't lie to Momma, no matter the circumstance. The words of the hell-preaching preacher had been dented in my memory. However, at the awakening of the scandal, I lost a piece of myself, the piece that knew the difference between a lie and the truth. After all, he had been living one big lie, so what was the truth anymore? Was there truth? The truth tunnel in my mind slowly deteriorated.

I had held an excruciating, horrible secret from that day when I was

thirteen years old. So, in a sense, I was holding a lie in my heart. When Momma made it home, she always checked on me before she went about her business. If I was up, I said I'd had a great day and was doing my homework all evening. The more I got away with it, the more it escalated. When Momma's work schedule changed, I had to devise a plan to spend time with Steve.

I was about to do the scariest and most drastic thing I had ever done. Of course, I thanked Andrea and Clara for being the source of the idea.

CHAPTER TEN

Road Trip 2014 Memphis, Tennessee

We arrived in Memphis late, and I was exhausted for some reason or the other, that all I wanted to do was sleep.

The Morning light rose high and the morning breath filled the atmosphere. It was another day I found myself grateful just to wake up, yet not fully remembering my dreams or if I even had a dream.

"How are you feeling this morning?" Patti asked. "Any withdrawal

symptoms? Shaking, weakness, or nausea?"

"You really think I'm a full-blown alcoholic, don't you?" Am I an

alcoholic or not? I didn't have anything to drink so far and I felt ok, so I didn't understand why people felt as though I was this drunk-slob.

Patti laid her magazine on her lap and sat upright with her back leaning on the head board. "That's not what I said. I'm merely using my experience to navigate myself through your recovery."

"I'm fine." I was rather annoyed.

Patti flung her covers and moved her legs and planted her feet on the ground.

"Great! They serve breakfast until ten, so I'll meet you downstairs after you take a shower."

* * *

Downstairs, in the hotel restaurant thirty minutes later, I looked at my watch patiently waiting for Nandi. It was nine forty-five. I had to flag down a waiter and order an omelet and dry toast to go for Nandi. She'd barely touched her dinner the night before, so I was really hoping she

would have an appetite that morning. When the waiter brought the to-go bag, I headed back to the room I was sharing with Nandi, *that girl had better be showered and dressed because we need to go over the day's plans*. I thought.

I inserted the key card in the door and crossed the threshold only to

find Nandi still underneath the covers.

"Nandi!" I shook her aggressively. "I thought you were getting ready to meet me for breakfast when I left the room?"

"I was..." Nandi mumbled.

116

"What?" I leaned closer to Nandi's muffled voice from behind the

covers to hear her closely.

"I said I was! Leave me alone." Nandi scowled.

I knew something wasn't right. I flipped off Nandi's covers and all of a sudden, I was hit with a familiar stench. "Have you been drinking?"

Nandi snatched back the covers and pulled them over her head.

"Go away!"

"Oh, my gosh, Nandi! I smell alcohol on your breath." I dropped to my knees to look underneath the bed. Finding nothing, I went into the closet and pulled out Nandi's bags.

Hearing the commotion Nandi peeked from underneath her covers. Nandi must have heard me going through her belongings, she jumped out of bed and stormed toward me. "What do you think you're doing?" Nandi shouted as she aggressively snatched the bag out of my hand.

My grip was stronger than that of a drunken Nandi, who could barely stand.

"Nandi! Let go of the bag!" I became quickly annoyed at her effort and I felt my chest heaving and my breathing became loud and deep. I usually got this way when my temper trigger had been ignited and it had been a very long time since I felt that way. I snatched the bag from Nandi's weak grip and dumped its contents on the bed.

"What are you looking for?" Nandi screamed.

"Back off, Nandi." I sifted through the belongings all while trying to shield Nandi from my way which made me feel as though I was playing professional defense for the National Women's Basketball Association.

"Have you lost your mind, Patti?" Nandi could barely hold herself up as she slurred her words.

I found what I was looking for and I held it up and it was an empty bottle of vodka. "You promised me!" I felt my skin boiling from within my body.

"I didn't promise you anything." Nandi hiccupped after her slurred speech.

"Where did you get this?" I was beyond furious. If anger had a barometer, mine would have been way over the normal reading.

Unfazed by my anger, Nandi stumbled back toward her bed and crawled under the covers.

"I got it from..." Nandi paused to belch and then laughed. "the store."

"You think this is a joke? Do you think this is for me or Brian?" I was very upset.

"No, and I don't care anymore."

The last time I felt this angry was in college and Nandi had just unleashed an emotion I did not care to surface, and I was afraid the next thing to come out of my mouth would bother her emotionally because I really didn't have anything nice to say. "One minute you say you want to change, and the next minute you binge on a big bottle of liquor. What do you want me to do? I'm getting tired of trying to help you if you don't want the help." My voice started to crack, I had to gasp for air, wiping

my nose I continued to talk. "Don't you see that you are way more than this thing?"

Nandi shrugged carelessly underneath the covers. "Maybe I'm meant to die like this."

Overwhelmed with pain and anger, I had to leave so I grabbed my

phone, my purse, my sunglasses, and my car keys and headed to my car. Once I was inside my car, I speed-dialed, unable to keep my overflow of emotions inside.

"Hello, beautiful," Pierre answered in his stern tone.

"I can't do this, babe," I said, trying to stop my voice from cracking.

"Do what? Is everything okay? Where y'all at?"

I took in a deep breath. "We're safe. We're in downtown Memphis. She's laid up in the hotel room, drunk as a skunk, and I am trying my best to help her."

"Honey, listen to me. Remember, this is your ministry. God orchestrated this ministry and you are in a spiritual warfare. Grab your Bible and let's read Ephesians 6:10-12. You should know this by heart."

I grabbed my Bible from the back seat and I opened it to the verse, we read it together.

"Finally, be strong in the Lord and in the strength of his might. Put

on the whole armor of God, that you may be able to stand against the schemes of the devil. For we do not wrestle against flesh and blood, but against the rulers, against the authorities, against the cosmic powers over this present darkness, against the spiritual forces of evil in the heavenly places."

"This is what your ministry is up against, spiritual warfare. It's easy to forget because Nandi is not one of your clients or members, but she is close and dear to you. Not only are you trying to help her, but you are also emotionally connected to her, and you want to see her healed and set free like others you have helped, right?"

"Right."

"Honey, God has ordained you for this. You've come too far to give up on her. She needs you. I know it might not seem like it, but she does. It's not Nandi you're up against. This thing that's holding her is spiritual, so you have to pray for the enemy to be loosed and for her eyes to see the truth."

"But I can't do this..."

Pierre interruptedly spoke. "Yes! you can...Listen to me. Once she

knows the truth, her heart can receive Jesus and her mind can accept deliverance. The enemy knows what you're doing, and he is trying to discourage your efforts. Remember, before you planned this trip, you and I fasted for thirty days for Nandi."

"Yes, we did, and God will honor that." As I remembered our sacrifice.

"Okay, then this is what needs to happen before the breakthrough.

Let's read verses 13-18 together."

Therefore, take up the whole armor of God, that you may be able to withstand in the evil day, and having done all, to stand firm. Stand therefore, having fastened on the belt of truth, and having put on the breastplate of righteousness, and, as shoes for your feet, having put on the readiness given by the gospel of peace. In all circumstances, take up the shield of faith, with which you can extinguish all the flaming darts of the evil one; and take the helmet of salvation, and the sword of the Spirit, which is the word of God, praying at all times in the Spirit, with all prayer and supplication. To that end keep alert with all perseverance, making supplication for all the saints.

"Amen! How are you feeling right now, babe?" Pierre said with a smile in his voice.

"Much, much better." I felt my heart slowing down to a regular pace

and my ears were not hot, so I knew I was cooling off.

"Good! Now understand that God is faithful. Do you believe Nandi

will be free?" Pierre Said.

"Yes!" I felt a gush of fire in my heart; almost like new hope.

"Do you believe Nandi will healed?"

"Yes!"

"Do you believe God will deliver Nandi from her bondage to alcoholism?" Pierre spoke with authority.

"I know God will set Nandi free, for the word says in John 8:36, 'So if the Son sets you free, you will be free indeed.' And I believe the word! The fire has just lit back up in my soul." I felt joy.

"I know how frustrating it can feel sometimes, and that is why you have to stay prayed up. I've been fasting from the day you both left, and I will continue until the day you get back. I talked to Brian the other day, and he's in agreement with me and is fasting with me. We get together each morning to pray for you and Nandi"

"Thank you, babe. I need all the prayers I can get."

"You're welcome hon. Before you go back in the hotel room, ask God to show you how to help Nandi and for the Lord's will to be done over her life. Come against the opposition. Plead the blood of Jesus over you and Nandi, and when you get back in the room, get your anointing oil out of your purse and anoint her forehead and pray for her. Anoint her bags, her clothes, and pray."

"I will. How has Brian been holding up?" I was hesitant to know.

"He's pressing through it. Before he joined me in the fast, he was ready to throw in the towel."

"No! Not divorce?"

Pierre sighed. "Yes, but joining me on this fast and in prayer has helped ease his mind a little bit."

"Thank goodness, because that would absolutely crush Nandi. I know she sometimes thinks she'd be fine without Brian, but I know she loves him and would be devastated if Brian went that route."

Back in the hotel room five minutes later, I found Nandi sound asleep and snoring. I took my bottle of anointing oil from my purse and anointed Nandi's clothes, shoes, and bags. Then I applied some oil lightly on Nandi's forehead, and Nandi didn't move. I kneeled beside Nandi's bed and whispered a prayer of love and thanksgiving. Then I began to pray for her.

"May your will be done in her life. Touch her tongue until she no longer desires alcohol and open her eyes to the truth. Heal her, save her, deliver her. Set her free to walk in Your will. Devil, I command you to get out of her body, out of her life, out of her mind, and off her tongue, in Jesus' name. Holy Spirit, ignite a flame of righteousness in Nandi's heart, in the name of Jesus. Amen."

* * *

Twenty-Three Years Earlier

I'll always remember my sophomore summer break. The besties and

I had finished another semester well. Despite Momma's feelings about

Clara and Andrea, we still hung around together closer than a doorknob to a door. Momma's punishment of banning me from them didn't stick.

When we came back to school to start our sophomore year, it appeared like we had never been apart. If it wasn't for Steve, I would have felt Momma's punishment more painfully, but Steve was a great distraction.

After Momma caught me with makeup on during the summer of our freshman year, she no longer trusted me. It was going to take a long time to gain a smidgen of it back. So during my sophomore summer break, I started telling Momma what I thought she wanted to hear. That way, I got to hang with Clara and Andrea and Steve.

Steve was now out of high school, attending a local college, and still worked.

I was the only one among my friends who still talked to the three boys from our freshmen year. Clara and Andrea changed boyfriends like a girl changes purses. I never understood what that was all about, but Steve still worked to my advantage as a great prop. I still had not felt a love bug for him, but I was comfortable with him and his ways.

Three weeks into the summer, I had barely seen Steve, but my girls kept me so occupied that I didn't obsess about him. That sophomore summer, Clara found someone to make fake college identification cards

for us. After the incident in the summer of my freshman year, Momma didn't want me to spend the night or hang out at Clara's home. So the only way I could hang out with them was to do what they had inspired me to do before. We spent the night at Andrea's house only one time the summer of my freshman year before Momma banned me from hanging out with them. Andrea wanted us to meet with James, Marcello, and Steve, so she devised a sneaking-out plan.

That would go down in history as the scariest thing I had ever done because Andrea's parents scared me straight. Their strict, stern ways would put any correctional officer to shame, but amazingly enough, this wasn't scary enough for Andrea. She always said, "Oh, well, if I get

caught, at least I had my share of fun."

With that kind of example, Clara and I jumped on the bandwagon like a couple of foolish teens. That night, we snuck out of Andrea's bedroom window and tiptoed out to the driveway, where James and the rest of the boys waited for us. My heart felt as if it was going to jump out of my chest. James drove us to the ice cream parlor and bought some cones. Then we went to the drive-in movie.

Everyone else seemed relaxed, loud, and giddy. I was tense, checking my wristwatch every few minutes to make sure it wasn't getting too late. By the time we headed back to Andrea's house, it was two o'clock in the morning. I had never been up and out that late, except for a few church events. The only times I had ever been out that late was for all-night prayers. James pulled up past Andrea's house with his headlights off. We got out of his car and took off our shoes. We avoided the driveway, but the neighbor's rowdy dog sniffed us out anyway and barked.

Clara screamed, apparently startled. We dashed through the driveway, and the garage light sensor switched on. The next thing we saw was Andrea's parent's bedroom light coming on. I had never been so scared in my life. I grabbed my chest to make sure my heart was still in there, but all I could feel were the aggressive palpitations of my heart.

We grabbed each other's hands and ran toward Andrea's window. The ferocious-sounding dog next door shook the frail fence while barking. I had never seen that dog before, but it sounded huge and ready to eat us up.

Andrea popped half of her window screen open and dove into her room as if she had done it before. Clara followed suit and, out of fear, I dove in too.

The room was dark, but I could hear Andrea's parents in the hall. Andrea quickly shut her window. Clara was already in bed, still in her clothes, shoes, and makeup. Andrea grabbed my hand and guided me to her bed, then she pushed me toward it and jumped in after me. She grabbed her cover in the nick of time and threw it over her head. I closed my eyes and faced the wall.

Clara was pretending to snore when Andrea's door flung wide open. I opened my eyes and all I saw on the wall was their imprinted shadows. I quickly squeezed my eyelids tight in hopes that when I opened them again, her parents would be gone, or I would find that this was all a nightmare. My nightmare theory vanished when the lights came on and all I could see was the pinkish color of the back of my eyelids.

Andrea's parents stood there whispering, and I whispered too, but mine were prayers. If they pulled back the covers, they would see that

we had been out. That would have been the last breath I would have taken here on earth, especially once Momma found out.

Andrea deserved an Oscar that night. She acted sleepy and disturbed

by the light, so her parents switched off the light and closed the door. Sweat beads dripped down my forehead faster than raindrops on a window. If dogs could talk; the neighbor's dog would have ratted us out that night. But, as scary as that whole experience was, it was exhilarating too, like a bad rollercoaster ride. And it helped me to discover the art of playing James Bond at home. Because of that, I managed to hang out

with Steve all summer after Momma was asleep.

Soon Clara had our fake college identification cards. Of course, we

immediately concocted a plan for the first time we'd use them. Since I couldn't spend the night at either Clara's house or Andrea's house, we decided that they would pick me up at home. By then, Clara had a car and a license.

We planned to hang out on a Friday night. Clara had heard about a college spot that was supposedly frequented by all kinds of cute college boys. So, that night, we synchronized our watches and waited for our 11:30 p.m. meeting time. Clara would park her car down the street from her driveway and wait for her grandma to fall asleep by 8:30. Then she would get ready and come out to pick me up first since we lived close to each other. We would pick up Andrea by midnight.

The first part of the plan worked. Once we'd picked up Andrea, we were off to a supposed great night, with not a care or concern in the world. My mind and heart had been hardened as coal, even the thought of being caught didn't bother me.

I don't know what made me act like a full-grown woman. But we hit the highway, jamming to our music. We had already role-played a couple of times, so we'd know how to act if security questioned our IDs. We weren't too concerned about it because Clara and her cousin had tried these fake IDs before with no trouble.

We finally arrived at a cheesy-looking club. The music was utterly
loud, and the outside scene was quite intimidating with real college kids hanging out on the curb. The lines to enter wrapped around the building, but that didn't stop three immature, determined teenagers from walking toward the door. Clara had her professional-wanna-be makeup bag. As she parked, she convinced me to get in the backseat while Andrea, who was already made up, went to stand in line. Clara was so good at what she did that my mini makeover session seemed to last only five minutes. When we were done, Clara handed me a

bag of clothes. By now, I was a pro at changing in the car. I slipped out of my pajamas and into the dress Clara gave me.

When Clara and I were done with the car makeup session, we joined

Andrea in line. This would be the first time I would ever walk through the doors of a nightclub. Clara had already coached me through and through. *Make sure you look confident. Straighten your shoulders, walk tall, and just smile or flirt with the security if he seems to take long looking at your ID.* If anyone had the ability to make you feel confident, it was Clara.

Soon we reached the front of the line. Andrea was first, I was in the middle, and Clara was in the back. I started to feel nervous when Andrea gave the security her ID. As he looked at it, he kept glancing over at me. Or maybe I was just paranoid. I surely hoped the makeup made me look that much older.

After looking at Andrea's ID, he signaled for her to enter. Then it was my turn. I walked slowly, mainly because Clara had given me a pair of her heels. I handed him my ID. He looked at it, he looked at me, he looked back at the ID, and he looked at me again.

By this time, my heart was thumping so hard and fast that if he stared long enough, he could have seen my chest heaving. I smiled and then he flipped the ID to look at the back. He pulled out a flashlight when a voice came over his shoulder microphone. The guard stepped to the side with my ID in his hand and responded to the shoulder mic.

Then he rushed back to me, handed me my ID, and waved me inside. He took off running into the club, and another security officer came to the door. That was a close one. Supposedly, a fight had broken out in the club and, as head of security, he had to attend to it.

When Clara was cleared at the door, she led us to our table. I must have died and gone to a different planet. People danced carelessly all around us. Some hovered at the edges of the dance floor, watching the live entertainment. With each step, we could feel the vibrations of the loud music in the soles of our feet.

We arrived at our table, sat down, and looked cute. A few boys tried stopping by to talk to us, but we were so preoccupied with the abundance of college boys, that we dismissed those who tried to get to know us. Clara and Andrea loved the attention and chose to use it to their advantage. I, on the other hand, played the part of having a boyfriend, even though Steve wasn't a real boyfriend.

Clara went to the bar and bought us some soft drinks. She made sure the bartender poured them into cocktail cups. We did not drink but we wanted to act as though we were grown, and we were drinking some fancy-schmancy cocktail. We sipped the watered-down sodas as though we were classy ladies.

Clara and Andrea ate up all the attention. I think they got it simply because of the itty-bitty skirts they had on. They had the guts to wear them, but I didn't. My dress was knee-length but still felt uncomfortable. It felt as though it had been spray-painted onto my body. Clara picked it out for me because she thought it brought out my supposed "curves."

This must have been Andrea's greatest payback. When she came back from the bathroom, she grabbed my hand. This wasn't a common gesture from her.

I followed her through the maze of human bodies until we got close to the restroom. By this time, Clara scurried along behind us, asking a hundred questions. When we got close to the restroom, Andrea pointed to the far corner. I looked because I thought she might have been trying to fix me up with someone. As I adjusted my focus, I recognized a familiar face, it was Steve.

My heart broke. Then I felt indignant. He had told me he was too

tired to hang out with me that evening and that storyline was going home to sleep. I knew I wasn't in love with the man, but he was my "boyfriend-prop." He had grown on me, and I was in deep like with him.

I felt frozen in time. My anger and tears accumulated at the same time. Clara grabbed my wrist and tried to pull me away from what was happening in the distance, but I wasn't having it. I needed to confront Steve in my pain.

Without rational thought, I walked toward Steve and stood next to him as he was in this girl's face. When he looked my way, his eyes widened. He knew he was busted.

I couldn't do anything but fold my arms in front of myself and give him an evil stare. The girl looked at me as if I had lost my mind, so I had to clear the air. "This is my boyfriend." That ought to do it.

She said, "We've been together for two years." Ouch! That was Information overload because the last time I checked he was my boyfriend.

Those words brought the club to a Jerry Springer moment. Clara tried to pull me away from them, and Andrea kept egging it on. Initially, I didn't have a problem with this girl. But then she got up in my face and started a yelling match. Steve totally disregarded me and tried to pull this drunk girl away from me.

Andrea was acting like a hype man on stage, stirring things up more and more. The next thing I remember was fists flying between Andrea and this girl. I knew Andrea was not defending me. She just loved to
fight whenever she got the chance.

The commotion escalated when this girl's friends jumped in. Clara and I tried to pull Andrea away, but by then, it was too late. Andrea had straddled the girl and was giving her the ultimate smackdown while the girl tried to cover her face. Andrea was so much in the moment that she didn't feel Clara and me trying to pull her off the girl. She also didn't feel the girl's friends kicking her in the sides.

The two girls were on the floor as though they were in a boxing ring.

As far as I could tell, Andrea was winning. Then all of a sudden, the big, buff security guards ran over and ripped the two apart.

CHAPTER ELEVEN

Continued...

T he day after the fiasco, I could hardly sleep. As soon as I finally fell asleep, I heard a loud knock followed by a gust of wind from the rapid opening of the door.

"Nandi Jean!" Momma hollered at the top of her lungs. "Get up right

now! You have some explaining to do, young lady!"

I hadn't seen or heard Momma that angry in a while. I was still in a sleepy daze, so as I got up, I tried to think of any chores I might have neglected that could have her fuming so hard on a Saturday morning.

"What?" I asked as I kicked off the covers.

"Who do you think you are talking to, little girl?" Momma paused in her huffing and puffing, then she muttered under her breath, "Lord Jesus, give me strength."

She leaned against the wall, hands folded in front of her chest and nostrils flaring. "I just got off the phone with Connie Mitchell. Is there something you want to tell me?"

The last name rang a bell, but the first name didn't. I was in a daze of exhaustion, my sleep robbed off by my thoughts. "Who?"

"Don't play games with me, young lady! Andrea's mother, that's who." Wow, was the room spinning? I almost had a heart attack in my teens. Then everything started moving slowly. Momma must have been talking about the previous night's events. I tried to come up with a good, sustainable lie, but I was too tired to think.

"Is Miss Connie okay?" My words rushed out before I had a chance to process them. But by the time they rang in my own ears, I knew I had to stall because, in my deepest gut, I knew where it was going. I wasn't ready to handle the wrath of Momma Jean.

"Don't play games with me, child. You know exactly what's going on."

"What are you talking about, Momma?" I loved giving her a blank

stare in her moments of seriousness.

"I am not playing games with you."

When momma got upset her big Bantu nose flared out and her eyes widened, the veins in her neck thickened with an indentation on her skin.

"Where were you last night?" Momma insisted while yelling.

If I hadn't been up before, I was by now. There was nothing pleasant about Momma's interrogation. I was in a conundrum. Since

I didn't know how much Momma knew, I needed to be careful not to say too much. My best strategy was to bait her and throw out misleading questions, so she'd tell me what she knew.

I should've known I'd need to wear my floatation device because Andrea wasn't the type to sit alone on a sinking ship. Everyone in it had to go down with her. She was the most vindictive person I ever met, and she had apparently decided I was to be the one to drown with her. As though making me watch Steve making out with that girl wasn't enough for her.

I shook off those thoughts and tried to concentrate on staying afloat,

with or without Andrea. Where was I last night? If I say I was at the movies, she'll ask what time I went, since I was supposed to be home. I had to say something, but not the club.

"Young lady, I am waiting for your response," Momma shouted.

I froze for a moment. "The movies."

By now momma was pacing up and down with her hands folded across

her chest. "That's not what Connie said."

"That's where we were...me and Clara." I cringed inside. Not only had I told another lie, but I brought Clara into this too.

"Connie Mitchell told me you were at that worldly college nightclub

with Andrea."

My mind raced in panic. "Me? No, ma'am, that wasn't me. You

know Andrea doesn't like me. She'll say anything to get me in trouble." I focused on the pink flannel sheet I'd kicked to the foot of the bed, unable to look Momma in the eye while telling a blatant lie.

Momma gave me the headshake of shame as her head shock from side-to-side. "Nandi! I told you about them little fast girls, but you don't listen to me. I wasn't born last night. I know you were down there with them."

I had no response. I was busted. Thanks to Andrea, I had no rebuttal to this case. Momma always took everyone else's word over mine, so I had already lost this case before she walked into my room. Yes, I failed her again. But I wished she would let me explain before she automatically assumed I was responsible for whatever people said I did. If a total stranger called and said I stole something, she would believe the stranger before asking me. That was our one-way relationship.

"I'm sorry, Momma."

Momma gave me the headshake of shame once more. "You're 'sorry' is wearing its course on me. This is not the way I raised you."

She gave me her sternest look, the one that always warned me something worse was yet to come. "You know better. You are never to communicate with Clara or Andrea again. Ever since the three of y'all got together, you've been nothing but trouble."

"It's not true, Momma!" The moment the words escaped my lips, I realized I must have lost my mind, interrupting Momma. But I was sick and tired of her blaming my circle of friends for my actions. No one forced me to do anything I didn't want to do. I freely went, without pressure from anyone. But Momma was in so much denial that she still viewed me as an innocent angel who was being corrupted by some *worldly girls.*

"Did you just interrupt me?" Momma cuffed my chin and tilted my

head back so she could look at me.

"No, ma'am. I'm sorry...."

"All that sassiness comes from hanging out with those unchurched girls." Momma released her grip and headed for the door. Then she looked back. "You are grounded for the rest of the summer. Get ready so I can take you to the library. All you are doing for the rest of the summer is reading and writing book reports for me." She stalked off and shut the door.

I would rather be in detention for the rest of my life than to spend time reading and writing book reports. That was the cruelest punishment I had yet received in my entire life. No friends and no Steve to take my mind off my punishment. Thanks to Andrea.

* * *

Road Trip 2014

"Rise and shine, sunshine." Patti seemed to be hollering right next to my ear. I turned over in my seat and adjusted the pillow under my head.

"How long have I been sleeping?"

Patti took a sip of her coffee before speaking. "About two and a half

hours. You must have been wiped out."

"I'm exhausted. I can't believe the sun is still up."

"We've only been on the road a couple of hours."

It really felt like we had been on the road longer than two hours.

"Where are we?"

Patti's voice piqued. "Take a guess."

"The middle of nowhere?" I rose from my reclined position to gaze out the window. All I could see was a field of goldenrod from afar.

"Oh, no. Please tell me we are not in Mississippi."

But I knew we were, and that realization made my heart pound harshly. Surely, we're not going to hang out in this dreaded state. I slammed on my sunglasses, the bright sun already giving me eye strain. What if Patti was taking me to Lois West's home? I feel as though I was still dreaming. I had agreed to be Patti's experiment for her group study, but I was not ready to face Mississippi again.

"Calm down, Nandi. We're heading over to Madison. I need to make

a little stop there, and then we'll be on our way."

"Madison! What for?" My stomach turned as if I'd eaten at a bad

Mexican restaurant. I didn't recall Patti ever saying she knew anyone in Madison. I didn't know anyone there, and I didn't recall Momma talking about that town either. I sensed a skunk in this plan.

Patti was up to something, and that bothered me. I had no idea what she was up to, and that made me even more uneasy.

"Trust me, Nandi." Patti leaned forward to turn up the volume on the

radio.

"Oh, my gosh! Turn it up some more." I sang along.

Patti interrupted the singing. "For a second, you sounded almost like Deniece Williams."

"My voice is kind of raspy right now, but I see you still have your sense of humor."

"Honestly, your voice is pretty."

"I sang soprano in the choir from a young age. It's not like I had a choice. Momma was the choir director for some years, and she insisted on having a strong soprano section. Even at the tender age of nine, I could hold a note for a full six measures, thanks to her."

"Well, one of these days, you'll be able to use that gift in a church choir somewhere."

What was she thinking? "Sure, whatever you say." All I know is that Momma Jean, with all her holy and sanctified talk, loved Deniece Williams. The first time I heard Momma play Silly in the house was right around the time she broke up with Mr. Kenny. Ever since then, I noticed a pattern. Whenever she went through a breakup, that song seemed to get her through it. I remember that, after my ordeal with Steve, all I wanted to do was listen to Momma's tape of that same song through my headset.

Absorbed as I was with early childhood memories, I couldn't help but recline my seat and trust my best friend. The name Mississippi had left a sour taste in my mouth because of the pain I endured at Lois's hand.

But I couldn't neglect Mississippi's magnificence as I saw it through my now-grown eyes. This place was pristine, modestly green, and clean. From afar and along the roadsides I saw some of Momma's favorite collectibles. Goldenrod still stood tall and fierce in front of all the dark-wooded green trees, adding color among weeds.

Some goldenrod grew sporadically, and others grew together, but their randomness on the side of the highway was perfect. And the black-eyed Susan's; if you saw one, you saw others. When we moved to the suburbs in Missouri, one of the first things Momma did was to plant some black-eyed Susan's in the backyard. During blossoming season, she spent all her free time feeding her plants, so they would grow. And grow they did. Momma was so obsessed by black-eyed Susan's, she decorated her kitchen with them.

Her wall borders had big, fancy cutouts of black-eyed Susan's, and the kitchen table linens were yellow and black. She purchased some fancy paper napkins that had black-eyed Susan's on them, and I was never allowed to use them. On the two-seater kitchen table surface, Momma
had black placemats and sunflower-yellow ceramic dinner plates.

Black bread plates sat upon them, and she arranged silverware wrapped up in the black-eyed Susan paper napkins, rolled up fancy and held tight by a golden napkin ring. The salt and pepper shakers sat in the center of the table, both with black-eyed Susan print on them.

Even the kitchen floor tiles and the towels that hung on the oven door

had black-eyed Susan print on them. Needless to say, I had become an expert in spotting black-eyed Susan's from afar. The GPS advised us loudly that our destination was on the right.

"What are you thinking about?" Patti asked as I pulled myself out of

my daydreams. My mind was still preoccupied with glorious moments of Momma and wildflowers, but I wanted to keep those to myself for now. Instead of answering, I continued to scan the horizon, looking for more yellow and black. Then we turned into a long driveway.

"Are we lost?"

"Why would you think that?" Patti laughed at what must have been

confusion on my face.

"Just the fact that we are pulling up to a grand estate. Neither of us

knows anyone who would live in a house like that in Mississippi. I just don't want to get shot for trespassing."

The sound of laughter filled the car. "Shot! Girl, please, you watch too much TV. It happens that I kind of know the owner of this home. Trust me."

We parked near the white-columned antebellum neoclassical home that looked like a plantation mansion. It was all intact and pristine, the exterior of the house was covered in a snow-white color without a dust of dirt on it, you could tell the owners must have gone to great lengths to preserve its prestige. Patti unfastened her seat belt and stepped out of the car.

"C'mon, missy. Let's go."

"Wait. How well do you know these people?"

Patti grabbed my hand. "I am not having a full-blown conversation

with you outside these people's home. That would look awkward. Besides, they're probably watching us."

"Give me a second. And I hope this isn't a crazy surprise. You know

how I hate surprises."

"What are you doing?"

Whoever it was we were going to see must have been someone of the well-to-do so I took the next necessary measure. "Fixing my hair."

"Your hair looks fine...Let's go."

Trudging up the walk, I passed the most perfectly manicured lawn I'd ever seen. The topiary was amazingly done, and the entire exterior of this house looked like something from a home magazine. And who knew grass could take on such art patterns?

The house sat far from the road, and the drive was U-shaped and made of cobblestone. Near the front doors stood an elaborate fountain. The last time I saw water dancing in a fountain like that was on the strip in Las Vegas.

As we approached the front porch, I decided that the occupants of the house had great taste. It took Patti and me a few moments to find the doorbell, mainly because we were wowed by the intricate details of the glass art on the beveled door. By the time Patti finally rang the bell, we could hear footsteps from afar, and then a silhouette appeared through the glass door.

"Who is it?" an elderly female voice asked between the echoes of a

tiny-dog bark.

"It's Patti and Nandi," Patti yelled back.

The front door eased open. The woman inside looked familiar, but I

couldn't place her. Slender and of average height, she looked absolutely stunning. If I didn't know better, I would assume Patti had brought me to an etiquette class, because the woman had the appearance of an etiquette teacher.

Her makeup was natural and complimentary to her features, her hair

was salt-and-pepper but mostly white in the front. Her French roll was full and had a perfect side bang that hung close to her right brow but was long enough to be tucked into the French roll, creating a slick, professional look.

She wore fuchsia lipstick that complemented her wide smile and white teeth. Her outfit shouted "presidential first lady," except she wasn't in the White House. She had to be older than she looked. I guess this is what rich people look like up close.

"Ladies, come on in." She said as though she was expecting us. We entered a foyer that was big enough to be a bedroom. She locked the door behind us.

"My name is Cecelia, but Nandi, you can call me Aunt Cecelia." Her voice cracked a bit as she approached Patti with a formal handshake.

"Aunt Cecelia?"

The woman paused and grabbed the glasses hanging around her neck. She slid them on and peered at me.

"Yes, you're Nandi. Look at you, all grown up." She hugged me tight and then stepped back, tears in her eyes. Grabbing me by the hand, she invited us into the living room.

The hallway to the living room was long and hung with photographs and oil portraits dating from fifty years ago to the present. One photo captured my eye. I had to stop dead in my tracks. "Is this Momma?" I couldn't help it but ask.

"That's Jean and that's you as a baby. You must have been about three years old." Cecelia paused and wiped a runaway tear drop from her cheek.

CHAPTER TWELVE

Road Trip 2014

Everything moved in slow motion, hindering my comprehension, as I grabbed the photo albums and sat next to this stranger who called herself my aunt.

"I'll be right back. I'm going to step outside to call my husband," Patti said.

As if the situation wasn't weird enough on its own, now the only person I knew in the house had just walked out and left me behind with the mystery lady.

"Move those cushions, honey, and scoot closer to me," Cecelia said.

Sitting next to her felt awkward because opening up to strangers isn't one of my areas of expertise. I got it that she was my newfound aunt, but I was still puzzled. One minute I was binge-drinking my sorrows away in a dingy downtown-Memphis hotel, and the next I was being waited on in a mansion in Madison, Mississippi.

Why had I allowed Patti to take me on such an adventure? Cecelia placed her drinking glass on the coffee table and turned her knees towards me. "I had been looking for you and your momma for the past thirty-seven years."

"Thirty-seven years?"

"You were only three years old the last time I saw you and your mother. That's when we took the picture in the hallway." Cecelia reached for some tissue and blotted under her eyes. "I didn't know if you were alive or what had happened. Lois neglected the correspondence, by the time we caught up with Lois you and your Momma had left her home and she didn't know where you were at as well. The only thing that eased my mind for a short time before I turned back to worry again was the next-door neighbors."

"Grandpa Thompson?"

"Yes! You remembered." Cecelia laughed.

"That man saved my life more times than anyone would ever know."

"He was an awesome man." Cecelia reached for her tea and sipped, then she used her tissue to wipe her lipstick stain from it.

I almost felt as though Cecelia was my missing link to the puzzle of my father, even though I was scared to ask her about my father, I was more fearful of her response. I waited for a few minutes to pass while we sat in silence before asking Cecelia the million-dollar-question.

"Do you know my father?"

Cecelia laughed. "Do I know him? Of course, honey." Cecelia stopped in mid-sentence and scooted all the way back on to the couch and gently laid her arm on the armrest. "Let me ask you something. Has your mother ever mentioned me?"

I hadn't anticipated that response. "Momma never talked much about her upbringing. The only person she spoke much about was her great grand mammy who taught her basic life lessons like sewing, cooking, and reading the Bible."

Cecelia repositioned herself and tucked her hands into her laps and laced her fingers together.

"Your mother went through a lot. Her own mother died while giving

birth to her, and because of that, your mother was raised by Imogene Hendricks. Imogene was her great-grand mammy."

Mr. Boe peeked into the room. "Are y'all doin' fine." He said.

Cecelia gracefully nodded her head and continued to talk. Cecelia paused to inhale and gently exhaled. "Imogene was a busy mammy, and she worked hard to provide for all four nieces and nephews plus your mother. Willie is the oldest and last we knew of him was years ago. We heard he was somewhere up north. Deidra was the second born, and she has since passed."

Cecelia stood up and walked towards her bookshelf. With her back turned toward me she continued talking.

"No one knows what took her life. Back then, everything was ruled as a heart attack, but Deidra was only in her early thirties when she passed, so I don't think it was a heart attack. Hedrick was next. Poor lonesome soul, he was different, always stayed to himself and drank like a fish." Cecelia's voice became louder as she continued to shuffle through her bookshelf. I couldn't help myself but to get up and help her look for whatever it is she was looking for.

"What are you looking for auntie?"

"I will know it when I find it, honey. Thank you." Cecelia said while rearranging and shuffling her books. "He was stabbed at a bar fight and died at age twenty-five. The poor thing never lived to repent and never lived to be sober enough to understand life. And the last we heard from Francine, she was in Alabama." By this time, Cecelia had stacked books on the floor, scooted some to different parts of the bookshelf. "No one knows where Francine is. Ever since her last two divorces, it's hard to track her down, and she's never come to see the rest of the family down here either."

Cecelia looked at me and said. "Help me down child," as she extended her arm to me. I grabbed her arm tightly and she gracefully went on her knees and started moving the books out of the lower shelf.

"Then we have your mother, Jean Marie, the youngest of all the children Imogene raised, but the most ambitious. Imogene tried hard to convince the other children to go to college and make something of themselves, but none of them did except your momma."

Cecelia released a warm laugh into the atmosphere and clapped her hands at what she had just said. "Your momma was young, ambitious, and pretty. Your momma's mammy was half Creole, from Baton Rouge, Louisiana, but her folks migrated to Mississippi too long ago for them to trace their lineage to Louisiana." Cecelia had managed to take the whole bottom shelf of books out and was flipping through them.

"I knew for a fact that your momma was going to be someone in life until she met Morris, your father. Your momma was married to Morris for four years. Your father came into the marriage with a son from his previous marriage."

"Wait a minute. A son?"

"His name is Morris Junior. Things didn't go well in your parent's marriage, which ended up in a bitter separation. In those days, the church and society frowned on divorce. It wasn't something a woman did naturally." Cecelia started to pack the books back on the bottom shelf.

"So, when your momma left your father when you were about three years old, Lois West and I went to pick up Jean and you in Mobile Alabama and brought y'all back to Mississippi with us."

Cecelia picked up a dusty looking encyclopedia and shook it aggressively and a vintage photo came flying out. "There you are!" Cecelia shouted with Joy. "Get me up, honey." Cecelia reached her arm up towards me and I helped her up. Cecelia fixated her eyes on the photo as she finished telling me the story.

"Then Lois asked your momma and you to live with her, even though I was ready to take y'all up north with me and Charlie. But Lois thought it wasn't wise to move a whole family of four up north without knowing how things would turn out."

Cecelia sighed, with her eyes still appended to the photo.

"We agreed that you and your momma would stay in Lois' care. But if I'd known then what I know now, I would've just moved y'all up there with me."

I scooted closer to Cecelia to take a peek at the photo. "Where is my father?"

Cecelia's eyes never let go of the photo. "Honey, I can't even tell you. Last I knew, he was in Alabama somewhere."

"What about my brother? How old is he? Is he still alive?"

Cecelia shrugged her shoulders. "I think he's still alive. I can't tell you where he lives. He was three years older than you. Your father was highly upset at the way your mother left him, so he made it hard for your mother and Lois to see Morris Junior."

"Who are all these people in the photo?" I inquired.

Cecelia wore a proud smile as she handed me the photo. "This here is your family. Your mammy, pappy, brother, Uncle Charlie and I." Cecelia placed the photo in my hands and placed her hand on my shoulder as she walked me towards the sofa. I couldn't take my eyes off this vintage nostalgic photo, the questions I had about my father's looks where all on the photo. Cecelia and I sat close on the couch and I couldn't take my eyes away from the photo as Cecelia continued to talk.

"For the longest time, your father and brother bounced around from state to state. I don't blame your mother for leaving him. I would've done the same thing if I'd been in her shoes, but Lois held a grudge against your momma for a long time because your father is Lois' only son. Lois thought if she took in your momma and you, she might be able to convince your momma to go back to Morris." Cecelia drew a sigh. "Lois was concerned because it looked bad for the small church where he preached."

* * *

I bent down towards the floor and reached for the jar of coconut oil and placed it on the bed. I started applying small portions of coconut oil in the back of Nandi's scalp.

I couldn't but notice the sudden silence Nandi grew.

"Are you okay?"

Nandi shrugged her shoulders. "I guess." She said solemnly.

I could tell something had been occupying her mind. Her sudden quietness often and her blank gazes every now and then.

"You guess what?"

Nandi huffed. "I guess I'm as okay as I will ever get. Everything so far is not quite linking up, I met a relative but only to find out she can die at any moment…I suppose the good part is, I had a visual picture of my father."

I picked up a wide tooth comb to create some more parts in the scalp for oil.

"I understand what you mean." I couldn't help it but release a sigh.

Gasp. "It's just…I don't feel much like talking." Nandi insisted.

"Okay." Given the circumstances, I didn't anticipate her new relative having such sad news, not what I would have liked for Nandi especially after the fact that her mother passed away not too long ago.

Nandi whispered. "I'd like to know how you and my supposed aunt Cecelia arranged this."

I had managed to oil the back portion of her head and I was lightly massaging the hair. I didn't think that moment would be the perfect time to tell her that It all started when Pierre was helping Brian clean out Momma Jean's home, they found an old box in the basement.

When they opened it, there were all kinds of papers on top. Pierre started going through the supposed papers and found Momma Jeans marriage license, Lois West's address, and several letters from Cecelia Worthington. In that same box was a family Bible that had a photo in it. The picture was of Momma Jean back in the day, and she was holding a little baby, whom we speculated was Nandi.

A man stood next to Momma Jean with his arm affectionately around her shoulder, and a little boy stood in front of him. Brian didn't know what to do since Nandi was still emotionally frail from the loss of Momma Jean. Brian asked Pierre to take the box with him to Chicago. After a couple of weeks, I borrowed his car and saw this filthy old box in the backseat.

I grabbed it, thinking it was trash. I started to go through it, the bottom came loose and the Bible hit the floor. Then a bunch of wrinkled papers followed. I picked up the Bible to flip through it and saw the picture. At first, I thought that was Momma Jean's brother or relative standing next to her. I started to read some of Cecelia's letters to Momma Jean, and then I saw the marriage license and it dawned on me that the man in the picture must have been Momma Jean's husband. I knew something had to be done because now I had questions.

I remembered that since college, Nandi always wanted to know more about her family, especially her father. So, I searched for Cecilia on Google and located her that way. I was ecstatic as though it was my family I was looking for. I talked to Brian, and he agreed that it would be great for the two of them to meet.

CHAPTER THIRTEEN

Road Trip 2014

I knew something was bothering Nandi and just from my past tendencies and recovery, I knew it would be rough for her I tried to do my best to keep a close eye on her.

"Nandi!" I yelled from behind her bedroom door. "Open up."

"Leave me alone!"

"Open the door for a second, please." I was becoming a little nervous not knowing Nandi's current state of mind so to calm myself down I paced up and down the hallway until I heard the door crack open. I stopped immediately, and Nandi stalked back to her bed without even acknowledging me.

"Look, I understand how everything is hard to deal with right now, but my main concern is your stomach. You didn't eat supper last night. It's almost 3:00 in the afternoon, and you still haven't eaten or come out of this room." I reminded Nandi.

"I know you hear me, and I want you to know that I'm on your side.   I am not your enemy. I came up here to tell you some good news."

"I don't want to hear any news," Nandi mumbled as she buried her head in the covers.

Sigh. "I understand." I sat down on the edge of the bed.

"You keep saying that, but I don't think you do." Nandi shifted positions while her head was still buried under the covers.

"I do understand but if you want to explain, then be my guest. I am all ears."

"My entire life has been a lie. One second, I hate the fact that Momma never told me about my biological father. The next minute, I can't hate my own mother, especially since she is six feet underground." Nandi uncovered her head. "I don't know how I feel about this man who is supposedly my father. Why did he take my brother and leave me and Momma Jean to fend for ourselves?"

I scooted closer to Nandi's head. "Stop right there. We don't know what took place back in that day. We can't make assumptions based on a picture or the little we know. However, it's natural for you to have mixed emotions. Maybe your father will be able to fill in the missing details since..."

"My father?" Nandi interrupted, her voice cracking. "I don't know if I want to see him or know him. Momma worked hard to help me get where I am, without his help, so why let him get involved in my life?"

I tried to pry the cover from Nandi's head so I can see her face, but her grip was strong. "Nonsense! Utter nonsense! You are filled with emotions right now, so I will let you sleep on it tonight and see how you feel tomorrow. I know that, deep down inside, you want to meet him. That's all you talked about in college. And remember how much money you and Brian spent doing that genealogy research and hiring an investigator to track your biological father? Remember that?"

"I remember, but..." With the back of her hand, Nandi wiped tears from her cheeks.

Little does she know... the truth of my life is; the year after I was saved, I wanted to confront my father. It wasn't easy since I knew only my mother's side of the story of his other family and his infidelity. I, too, had mixed feelings. My guard was up, keeping me from forming a relationship with my dad.

Although he lived at our address, he wasn't physically present most of the time. For years, I drowned my emotions in my sex addiction because I couldn't face the fact that I hated and resented my own biological father.

That knowledge was too difficult to handle with a clear mind. At that time, I didn't know that was what I was doing. But after I was delivered and had learned a little about addictive behaviors, I discovered I was trying to fill the void that my father's love was supposed to fill. I looked to men to accept me and to love me. The only way I thought I could love a man was to give them what I thought they wanted, which was sex. Because that door had been opened through the channel of molestation by my uncle, I found my flesh desiring sex more and more. As I continued to think about my father's ways with my family, I began to hate him.

I blamed my sex addiction on my father because if he'd been at home with Mom and me, his brother would never have violated me and taken my innocence. When my life spiraled out of control and I surrendered to Christ, I couldn't understand why I was still bound to thoughts of sex, or why I couldn't forgive my father. I prayed and cried for God to help me forgive, but I couldn't.

All day long, I told God I forgave my father, but I still had a knot of hate in my heart. I knew this because I still avoided him. Months later, God laid it on my heart to visit him. I was so torn that I couldn't bring myself to see him. So I ignored God's prompting and decided it was a crazy thought. But the more I tried forgetting that thought, the more it tugged at me. Finally, God used my husband. Pierre surprised me with a single ticket to England to visit my parents.

I knew then that it was time. I hadn't told Pierre what God laid on my heart, so I knew it was meant to be. I prayed the whole way there.

I wanted peace. I phoned my mother and told her I was coming for a brief visit, and she was elated. When I arrived at the airport, both my parents were waiting for me. My father came toward me first, and when he hugged me, he started to cry and asked me to forgive him. Each time he repeated his plea, his grip tightened on me. Then something shifted in the atmosphere. I cried as I never had before.

That load lifted off my shoulders. I felt lighter and suddenly, during a busy airport, an illuminating peace came into my heart. I knew that was what God wanted to happen. I didn't want to confront him about anything anymore. If I had left England that day and never learned why my father had another family, I would have gone in peace. I was satisfied. I had officially forgiven my father. I was freed from unforgiveness.

During my visit to England, mom came in my room, she looked dismayed and I thought she was going to mope and cry about my father's ways as she had always done before. I braced myself because I didn't want any more information about my father. I didn't want it to take away from the love and forgiveness I had just restored.

She sat in the rocking chair by the window and started to rock while gazing out the window in a creepy silence. Every now and then, she glanced at me as I packed. Then she gazed down as though in shame, and then back out the window as though in thought. Mind you, the whole time I was home, she kept to herself as though she had something on her mind. I knew that if it was crucial enough, she would tell me.

If she didn't, I didn't want to pry because my mother is a big-time pity-seeker. But this night, she got my attention. I stopped packing, sat on the edge of the bed, and asked her what was the matter. I knew I might regret those words. I didn't know if I was ready to hear what was on her mind. I didn't want anything to dampen my mood. At first, she said it was nothing, so I stood up to continue packing. Then she must have changed her mind.

Her Haitian-British accent thickened as she told me to sit down. The tone of her voice told me the news was not going to be good. I sat down in anticipation and fear. I honestly thought the worst that could happen in that moment was for her to tell me she was not my biological mother. I'd already heard the worst; the divorce threats, the unhappy tales of a mother whose husband had gone AWOL from home, the heartache my father caused her, and so on. But she had come up with something new to take me down from my happiness high.

My mother told me something had been in her heart for the longest time. When she said it was time for her to come clean with me, she scared me. I was too anxious to let her beat around the bush, so I asked her if she was dying. if she was not my mother. Then she asked me to forgive her for what she was about to tell me, and I freaked out. Had she committed a crime? My irrational thoughts became vibrant in my mind. I was getting ready to tear up when she sprung the news on me like an anchor-woman reporting breaking headlines.

She proceeded to tell me she wasn't entirely honest with me about my father. I felt as though I was on the Jerry Springer stage and she was getting ready to unleash the unthinkable on me. I thought she was getting ready to tell me that the man I had just forgiven at the airport and loved wholeheartedly again was not my biological father.

Mom rocked back and forth in the chair as she stared at me with blank eyes for a moment. Then she started to babble, telling me she was young and didn't know any better. If she'd had another chance, she would not do it again. She grew up in poverty back in Haiti and wasn't going to live like that in London. I could tell she was about to unveil something outside my measure of belief. You know trouble is coming when an individual starts a conversation by bringing up what they should've, could've, and didn't do. Deep insight was on the way.

Her parents feared for her life. They thought London would be too much for her to handle, and her older brothers envied her and put her down at the same time. They told her she wouldn't last a month in London before she'd return to their island. She was nothing but a small-time, country island girl, and the city would eat her alive. Because of their discouragement, she set her mind to make it in London. She refused to fail and let them be right.

After she arrived in London, she got in touch with the Haitian community and bounced around like a soccer ball from one family's home to the next. It was hard for families to take care of themselves, let alone a stranger. She worked odd jobs to make ends meet, but the money was only enough to pay for her lodging and a little food. She lasted six months in London, all on her own.

Every time she managed to call Haiti, she fabricated a story of success, even though she was miserable. She didn't want her parents to worry so she stayed strong. Then she met Francine. Francine was an elderly Haitian woman who owned a maid-services company, and she offered mom a job. She was a kind woman and took mom under her wing, caring for her like a mother.

They had an impressive clientele list, serving the elite of London. Mom marveled every time they worked in a mansion, and she pretended she was cleaning her own house. She knew that she would someday live in such a house and have such a lifestyle. But she didn't know that would happen sooner than later. The biggest home on moms list belonged to my father, Sean-Paul Barbeau.

Mom wondered why a single man had such a big house, but that was none of her business. One day, Francine couldn't make it to Mr. Barbeau's home, so mom had to go alone. Francine warned mom that he was a bit of a flirt. That was okay because my mother just wanted to go in, do her job, and leave.

Besides, he was always gone when they got there to clean. The butler let her in and she cleaned with all her heart, enjoying her freedom. Then she turned around and there was a tall Haitian-British man, staring at her. He insisted she continues and not mind him, and she tried her best to do so. But he followed her from room to room, and when she had finished cleaning, he paid her and added a very generous tip.

From that day on, he made subtle advances, but mom remained professional. Finally, he asked her out. At first, she was taken back, even though she knew he had an interest in her. She told Francine about it. Francine discouraged mom from dating him because she'd heard through the grapevine that he had a wife and children back in Haiti. However, mom thought Francine was jealous, like her brothers, who wished her failure. Besides, she thought that if it was true, she would have seen pictures of his family, since she'd been cleaning his home for months.

I hugged Nandi's spare pillow to my chest as I leaned back against the headboard beside her. Debating in my mind what I wanted to share with Nandi and what would be beneficial information to share with her. I knew overloading her with my family dysfunction wouldn't be enough to encourage her to meet her father.

I drew a deep breath and tightened my grip on the pillow all while in deep thought of this caption of my family's "dysfunction." I always knew my mother was strong, but for the first time in my life, I saw her weakness as she prepared herself to tell me her secret. By then, I had imagined the worst of a bad situation. She rocked back and forth, gazing out the window. Then suddenly, in a frightened, cold voice, she sprang it on me. She had made a crucial mistake out of selfishness and pride. She didn't want to believe

Francine when she'd said my father was married, so she ignored all the red flags that popped up like the overextended trips he took to Haiti while they were dating.

She justified the fact that he never took her with him to Haiti. She was not going to fail. She thought she'd found a great provider. She fell in love with my father for all the right reasons, but because he was a man of great status, she was automatically drawn to security like she had never seen. She became pregnant with me and my father married her.

This was her proudest moment. But my father was absent throughout her pregnancy, and I was born while he was in Haiti. Then she told me that all these years, she'd told me lies. I was so confused, until she told me the truth. Apparently, my father was married to a woman in Haiti, and my mother was his mistress. And worse, she knew it was true but she became pregnant on purpose, thinking he would surely marry her and leave his wife and children for her.

I was at a loss for words. All those years, I was bitter at my father for not being with us, when he was with his real family. Then I realized that my mother was a homewrecker! What was going on? This was not what I traveled to England for. My head spun out of control as I tried to process the information. Then she begged for my forgiveness. All I remember asking her was how he could be married to two women. Apparently, in Haiti, he had a traditional marriage to this woman. In England, he and my mother had a court marriage.

She feared that I wouldn't forgive her, but the bare truth was that he was a great man caught up in a love triangle. He tried his best to put his children first.

Mother said that after they got married, Papa spent more time in Haiti. She was crushed because she thought giving him a baby would draw him closer to her and would make him leave his Haitian wife and family. But it only made him spend more and more time in Haiti. And she used her hurt and pain to win my love and affection. She said she did that because when I was five years old, her folks back in Haiti heard about her.

They disowned her, as she brought shame to her maiden family name. Haiti was a small island, where most people knew each other. My father's wife found out about my mom and confronted my grandparents. She asked my mom's parents to talk to her into leaving Papa alone. Because of that humiliation, my mother vowed never to go back to Haiti. And because of her hurt and pain, she said nasty and mean things about my father to me, causing me to believe my father was a trifling, two-timing, sleazy dog.

I told my mother I needed time to process all the information she'd given me. I extended my stay and retreated into isolation that evening, nursing my mixed feelings. I love my mother dearly, but I was mad at her for lying to me about my father and not revealing her own selfish choices. I was hurt at the thought that I was nothing to her but bait. I started to wonder if she even loved me.

Perhaps she was being selfish, hoping still to win my father's whole heart. I didn't come out of my room that whole night and the next day. I asked God to reveal to me the meaning of my emotions. He came through, laying truth in my heart: That is why you came with a

willingness to forgive. Subtle and small was the Lord's voice in my heart. I got up from my bed and lifted the Lord's name in prayer. As I cried, the chains of anger, hate, and unforgiveness toward my mother came loose.

I knew then that God didn't send me there only to forgive my father. He also sent me there to forgive my mother and to pray for her. Those were by far the hardest twenty-four hours of my life.

Several moments had passed by that we'd been sitting in Nandi's room in silence when all of a sudden, Nandi whispered with hesitation and weighing her words with caution for their implication.

"You know what? I think I want to meet my father."

I gasped and was trying to contain my excitement. "I know it will bring you long-awaited closure. You've been missing that for a while, and you at least deserve to know more of your background, since Momma Jean's gone."

"You're right." Nandi sighed. "What else do I have to lose?"

She was right, she had nothing at all to lose. I am at a point in my life where I am purposely choosing to let things go before they grow bad fruit. Am I ashamed to be the child of a mistress, a homewrecker? Yes, I am, but that doesn't mean I love my parents any less. Do I regret anything about who I come from? I have no control over that, so no, I don't.

I am the person I am today because of who I came from. I chose my husband carefully because, even without knowing that my mother was a mistress, I purposely decided not to have a silent, miserable marriage like hers. The grass was not any greener on my side, just because I technically came from a two-parent home. But something in me wouldn't allow me to tell anyone about my family dysfunction.

Nandi has no idea on how blessed she is. Sometimes we all look at other people's lives and draw a picture from what we know or see, but if I'd told you that I would rather have grown up in a home like Nandi's she wouldn't believe it.

I love and respect my parents, but even without a father figure, Nandi had the genuine love and support of her mother. She had a different method of raising her, but she loved her and was involved in all aspects of her life. Momma Jean might not have raised Nandi the way she desired, but she gave her the fundamentals she needed, like church and school. She gave her a sound foundation.

My parents did the best they knew how for me too. When I met Nandi, she thought I was spoiled and stuck-up. But when she got to know me, she understood I was far from the imagery she saw. I used to want to grow up normal, under the radar of high social class. I yearned for an average life, one without glitz and glamour.

My father was gone physically and emotionally, and my mother was gone mentally and emotionally. She spent most of her time making sure I was in illustrious after-school activities, so she could chit-chat at tea time with her all-girls club, the Who's Who of Europe. I spent a lot of time bouncing from boarding school to boarding school.

When I was home, I went to etiquette class, equestrian training, swimming lessons, chess lessons, and forced play dates with the other socialite's children. I would trade all that for an average, normal, grounded life.

No one knows what it's like to lie in bed and hear the two people you love the most, my mother and father arguing and physically fighting. I used to put my pillow on my head, blocking out my mother's bloodcurdling screams when the physical fights broke loose.

The pillows muffled out a little of the sound, but it didn't help with the nightmares I endured every night. You wouldn't want to be raised in a home where the word 'love' was used only for the holidays and affection was desolate. Suddenly, the room's cold silence was swept away by a knock at the door.

CHAPTER FOURTEEN

Mississippi 2014

Cecelia entered the room without waiting for an invitation, and for some surprising reason, that didn't bother me at all because something about her spirit reminded me of Momma Jean. Aunt Cecelia had a graceful small contagious laugh she did that convinced me in her former life she must have been an etiquette teacher.

"Who is your husband, and where is he?" I asked with so much audacity.

"I knew that issue would surface sooner or later." Cecelia drew a long, winsome breath. "My late husband-Charlie is Lois West's half-brother. Your biological father is Lois West's son and only child."

An uneasy feeling crept up on me from the inside. "Wait! Do you

mean to tell me Lois West was my grandmother all this time?"

Cecelia sighed as she looked away. "Technically, yes." She hesitantly said.

So, I should say I was very surprised by this discovery. Never in a million years would I have ever thought I was related to her. "What do you mean, 'technically?'" I needed clarification. It was one of those moments where I heard what she said but I still wanted her to repeat it again hoping my brain could get extra time to process all the information.

Cecelia had her head down as she spoke in a lowered tone. "I know she didn't seem like a grandmother to you, and I am sorry for that." "Sorry for what?" I couldn't help but ask. She wasn't there.

Cecelia raised her head and looked at me. "I told my husband we
needed to take the two of you up North with us." Cecelia hesitated.

"God bless his soul, he was just never the confrontational type. At that time, we were newlyweds, and I didn't want to drive a wedge between Charlie and his half-sister, Lois." "That's understandable auntie." I said.

"They grew up apart. Lois's mother was initially married to Charlie's father until Lois' mother died during childbirth. Some years later, Lois's father married Charlie's mother, and Charlie was born. He had pleasant childhood memories, but Lois would beg to differ, especially after her mother passed. Lois claimed that Charlie's mother was mean to her, but in reality, her biological mother was physically abusive and unloving to her from the time she was born."

I adjusted myself to sit upright on the edge of the bed close to Cecelia. "It's making sense now that you mentioned it."

Cecelia shrugged. "Charlie's family thought Lois was a troubled, defiant kid, and that's why she never got along with Charlie's mother. Lois grew even more bitter and distant when her father passed. He left all his property, land, and money to Charlie's mother."

"Wow! That must have hurt." It felt like this discovery of Lois was getting that much more interesting. I reached over to the nightstand to take a sip of water.

Cecelia walked to the bathroom and reached under the sink and pulled out a hand towel as she spoke. "That will was the straw that broke the camel's back. After the funeral, Charlie didn't see Lois again until way later in life. I'm pretty sure Lois had bitter feelings about it. For all I know, something troubled her deeply. I never could quite put my finger on it."

I walked towards the bathroom. "It's all making sense to me on why

she was the way she was even though it shouldn't be an excuse."

Cecelia nodded her head in agreement. "For years after Lois surfaced with her son, she harassed Charlie, wanting a share of the land, properties, and money that was willed to his mother. Lois felt it all belonged to her and her son. Charlie never gave her anything, and she became even angrier. I knew something wasn't right in her spirit."

I couldn't contain my ill thoughts of Lois. Cecelia dried her hands on the hand towel. "Oh, honey. I used to tell Charlie all the time, but he was quick to dismiss my thoughts on her. Probably because of guilt over what his father did."

How many more surprises would this so-called aunt have for me

today? "What did you think of Lois?"

Cecelia let out a pretentious loud laugh. "Oh, honey, through deep

spiritual discernment, I knew for years that something was not right. I wondered how you and your momma were doing in her care. My concerns were confirmed when we finally moved back to the South and Charlie and I stopped at Lois's house."

"That must have been when Momma and I had just left or something."

From the bathroom, Cecelia grabbed my hand and led me to the foot

of the bed and sat down with me. "Yes. You and your momma were gone, and Lois claimed she didn't know why. But as Charlie and I left

Lois's home that day, we ran into Mr. Thompson."

Grandpa Thompson! My all-time lifesaver. "I loved that man."

Cecelia drew a pleasant smile. "A true man of God he was. He gave us your address in East St. Louis, but by the time we got there, y'all had already moved. Charlie and I looked for you two, but no one knew where y'all had gone. This lets me know that Lois West had been up to no good because it was not like Momma Jean to fall off the face of the earth." Cecelia's voice faded as she lowered her head and shook her head.

Lois West. Who'd have thought her name would ever come up again? Especially now.

Cecelia inhaled deeply and exhaled. "I'm sorry, Nandi, for leaving you and your momma the way we did," her eyes brimming over with compassion.

"It's okay. Things happen and that is life." It's good for me to know

that I am ok today. Now even though I know if Lois was standing here in front of me today I would feel very differently about her. "I just never understood..."

"Never understood what?" Aunt Cecelia asked.

I couldn't hold my tongue. No use causing more pain.

"Nothing." I couldn't say it.

Aunt Cecelia turned to place her hand on top of my hand. "You can

tell me, baby."

I changed a quick glance at Patti who had been sitting on the Bay window looking at aunt Cecelia and I like a tourist watching a tourist site. So much had already been revealed today, I might as well finish the job. "I never understood why Lois was so mean to me. I tried calling her grandma L like the neighborhood kids did, and boy, she tore up my butt with a belt just for saying that." I had to stop talking because that name was enough to cause tears on the cusp of my eyelids.

Cecelia squeezed my hand. "That wasn't your fault, baby."

I felt the tears streaming down my cheeks. "Whose fault was it then?" "Oh, honey." Cecelia scooted close to me and directed my head to her chest, seeming to struggle to hold back her tears. "It was no one's fault. She grew up in a violent home, and she was violent toward her son and you too. She didn't know any other way."

"She beat me if I didn't finish all my food. She beat me when I went outside to play. She beat me when I looked at her. She beat me for no reason!" Cecelia rocked back and forth as she stroked my head. "I wish I had known that then. I wish I could have helped."

I couldn't stop crying. I felt an enormous amount of heaviness in my throat and chest. "No one can say anything to take away the pain that evil woman caused me. I'm still afraid to sleep in the dark, because of some nights, when Momma was out late, I woke up to a cold leather belt striking me across my back, neck, arms, and face."

All of a sudden, I couldn't stop the tremor that started in my spine and worked its way down my arms and legs. "I thought I was an awful child because I spent most of my childhood being beaten by Lois. I can't understand how she can be my grandmother and yet treat me the way she did. She treated me as though we were no relation. Even a step-parent will treat their step-child with much more love and dignity than Lois gave me."

"I know, honey..."

I jerked my head away from Cecelia. "How do you know? You were not there!"

"I'm sorry, honey. Please forgive me." Cecelia broke down in tears.

Patti handed Cecelia and I some tissues and walked back to the bay window to sit down.

"My life is so messed up! I lost the only person who ever genuinely loved me. I am trying to deal with these emotions without alcohol for the first time in a long time, and it's not easy. Every night, I have nightmares about the things I never wanted to face sober. And now, here we are, talking of the woman who paved the road of hurt and pain in my life."

Cecelia squeezed my hand. "It's time to regain your freedom!" Cecelia said with boldness.

"I just don't want to hear another 'sorry' from anyone. I've made it thirty-nine years without an apology, and I plan on making it the rest of my life without anyone's apology or sympathy."

Cecelia laid a pillow on her thighs and lowered my head to it. I couldn't help myself but to lay like a newborn baby on this fluffy pillow as Cecelia softly rubbed my back, Cecelia signaled for Patti to hand her the throw blanket which she used to cover me. Then she started whispering a familiar song, oh how I had wished to be laying on Momma's laps one more time. Patti sat on the other side of the bed and joined Cecelia in the song:

Alas! And did my Savior bleed And did my Sov'reign die?

Would He devote that sacred head For such a worm as I?

At the cross, at the cross, where I first saw the light,

And the burden of my heart rolled away, It was there by faith I

received my sight, And now I am happy all the day!

Thy body was slain, sweet Jesus, Thine—

And bathed in its own blood—

While the firm mark of wrath divine, His soul in anguish stood.

Cecelia and Patti repeated the song over and over. The louder they sang, the louder I cried, and the louder I cried, the louder they sang.

"Why did Momma have to die?"

"Rest up, my child. Your soul is troubled." Cecelia stroked my hair while Patti continued to sing.

I felt in that moment I was fed up with living like I was. Life seemed so overwhelming. "I don't want to live anymore."

That brought out a rise in Cecelia. "Devil, you are a liar! I cast you out of her head in the name of Jesus. You have no dominion over her life because of the blood of Jesus!"

The more my mind dwelt on my life the more I felt defeated. "I can't go on with life, Auntie. I just can't. I've failed myself, my mother, and my husband. I have failed, period."

"Nonsense!" Cecelia yelled.

Immediately, Patti went into a loud prayer, and Cecelia started praying with Patti.

* * *

Early the next morning, I felt like I had been ran over by a train my

whole body was in pain. I sat straight up in bed. Had last night been a dream? "Aunt Cecelia?"

"Shh. It's going to be okay." Aunt Cecelia stood from the recliner next to my bed.

I was looking around to figure out if it was a dream or reality.

"What's going on?" Cecelia spoke half awake. "I think you were having a bad dream, dear."

"It was bad."

"In the name of Jesus, I bind and loose the yoke of infirmity and evil

illusions from Nandi's life," Cecelia said with confidence.

I still felt tired. "What time is it?"

Aunt Cecelia glanced at her watch. "It's 4:30 in the morning."

"I've been sleeping that long?" I reached over for the glass of water on the nightstand. "I dreamed ..."

Cecelia was going in and out of sleep in the recliner. "What is it,

honey?"

"Nothing. You don't have to sit up here with me all day."

Cecelia smiled with her eyes shut. "Yes, I do, honey. We are in this

together."

"I don't get it. What are we in together?"

178

"Nandi, you don't know much about me, but you can count on me being by your side every step of the way. One look at your face told me you have a troubled mind and an unrestful soul. I love you, and the devil is after you. But he's going to have to knock me down to get to it because I won't let him win." Cecelia pulled her throw over the blanket to her knees.

Cecelia got up and retrieved a Bible from the nightstand drawer. She sat beside me on the bed. She flipped through the thick book for a moment. "Here we are. John 8:36 says, 'If the Son, therefore, shall make you free, ye shall be free indeed.' If you believe Jesus died for your sins on the cross and you personally ask Him to come into your heart, you can be set free. God has much in store for you. Otherwise, why would

you struggle with your flesh's desires?" Cecelia paused and glanced over at me, I was in tears.

"God wants to set you free. You were not created to live a miserable life. We serve a living God who can heal you from the inside out." Cecelia leaned over to the nightstand and grabbed the box of tissues and offered me a tissue. "Sure, Lois planted a distasteful seed of deceit in your life, and throughout your life that seed has grown so much that it brought chaos. But now you stand a chance of starting over, starting afresh and cleansed in the blood." Aunt Cecelia gazed at the ceiling as she closed her Bible and laid it on her lap.

Start over? How many times had I already done that? What would be different this time? I was speechless. I pulled the covers over my head and pulled up my knees into a fetal position.

Cecelia cleared her throat. "I have something to share with you."

"What is it?" I was hesitant in response because I didn't know if my mind could process any more information.

"Your great-uncle Charlie was not saved his whole life. Matter of fact, he was a full-fledged heathen when I met him. But you know what?"

"What?"

Cecelia smiled big. "I knew there was more to him than his captivity. And I knew he came into my life for a reason. Now, mind you, I was saved as a young girl. When I met Charlie, I knew better than talking to an unsaved man, so I prayed and interceded for him." Cecelia grabbed a tissue from the tissue box and wiped the single escaped tear from her cheek.

"At that time, he was harassing me and trying to date me, but my momma and I were not having it. I decided to get up early every morning, get down on my knees in my room, and wail before the Lord. I didn't know what initially drew me to pray for him, but now I know it was the Holy Spirit." Cecelia groaned as she rubbed her hand on the Bible that was on her laps.

"I didn't like Charlie, but I prayed for a whole year, and then Charlie started coming to our church. I knew then that the effectual, fervent prayers had set him free. Your great-uncle Charlie went from

being a drunk and tobacco-smoker to a preacher at our church."
Cecelia gazed at the cover while plucking the lent off the cover.
"After that, he asked for my hand in marriage, and I accepted
without a doubt. You see, God had been preparing me to intercede
for Charlie's bloodline. The strongman of alcohol is deep-seated in
your father's bloodline. It had taken root generations ago and it
continues in that line today." Cecelia raised her
voice in excitement.

"I want to break and dismantle the strongman of addiction in
your bloodline, Nandi. Just like Charlie, you can be set free. Now, I
don't know what all is going on with you, but I know what the Spirit
has revealed to me. This is no second-hand information."

I turned towards my aunt, questions bombarding my mind. Was
this
possible? Could Aunt Cecelia pray for me as she had for Uncle
Charlie? Could I be set free?

Cecelia softly shook my shoulder. "Your infirmities and
strongman are hindering what God has for you. You might have
tried taking your life a couple of times, but you didn't succeed
because God has greater plans for you. Your addiction has held you
in bondage from the truth, but God says you, like Charlie, will be
set free!"

CHAPTER FIFTEEN

Road Trip 2014 Alabama

About three hours after Aunt Cecelia announced we were going to Alabama to see my father, the female voice of the GPS told us we had reached our destination. Patti pulled the car into the drive. The house was a small ranch-style that almost looked abandoned, with its grass long like a national park's. In it lay bits and pieces of bicycle parts, dolls, and other toys.

The front porch was stacked high with boxes on top of boxes, as though the garbage truck hadn't been to that house in years. On the other side of the house in the grass close to the driveway was two rusted old mobiles whose tires looked like they hadn't tasted tar in years.

"I'm as apprehensive as you are," Aunt Cecilia said.

I doubted that was possible. "I still can't believe we're here."

"I didn't want you to come at all, but the Lord has been dealing with me about this whole proposal." Aunt Cecelia held her hand on the seatbelt for a moment as if she still wasn't sure. "I'd rather protect you from anything you might find out here, but now I realize I can't make that decision for you."

I hadn't seen Aunt Cecelia nervous like this since meeting her. She seemed like a very cautious person and weird enough I was more concerned about her than her concern for me.

Aunt Cecelia's voice had a little quiver. "He doesn't expect us, so I

want to pray before we go knocking on the door." Aunt Cecelia bowed her head.

After praying, we sat in silence for a moment. Then I smoothed my

hair and checked my lipstick in the compact mirror. "Are you ready to go?" Aunt Cecelia asked as she finally pushed the seatbelt button. When we had all exited the car, Aunt Cecelia led the way up the porch stairs. At the door, she raised her hand to knock. She paused before her knuckles touched the door, then she gave a soft knock. She waited a whole three seconds and then announced, "No one's home." Patti pushed her way to the front of the door.

"Let me do it." Patti knocked harder and longer. A groggy-sounding, bass voice answered. "All right, all right, all right. I'm coming!"

The door flew open and there stood an unfamiliar, barefoot woman. Although it was two in the afternoon, she wore a moth-eaten morning robe that looked as if it used to be white but had lost numerous fights with the stain remover. It didn't take much thought to realize that she had received the bass in her voice through prolonged smoking. It was so deep that, if I had been talking to her on the phone, I could easily have mistaken her for a mister.

She had a pear-shaped body that stated, "No healthy lifestyle ever lived here." She had noticeable facial hairs, and it was hard to guess her age, since her wrinkles seemed due to a rough life, as opposed to age. This woman was every bit of 4 feet 11 inches tall. Her teeth were discolored, most likely from smoking and coffee, but she was not ashamed to smile through the discolored teeth and the rotted ones too.

"Isn't it early in the week for y'all to come out?" the lady behind the

bass voice said through the screen door.

"Were you expecting us?" Aunt Cecelia asked.

The lady forced a laugh. "I never anticipate y'all." She coughed as though she was coughing out a hair ball. "Y'all godly witnesses, right?"

Aunt Cecelia burst into laughter. "No, we're looking for Morris West. Does he live here?"

All of a sudden, the bass-voice lady dropped her smile and narrowed

her g gaze. "Who wants to know?" "His daughter," I said.

The lady looked at our faces one at a time as though taking a scan of

our faces to store in her brain zip-folder as she opened the screen door.

"Daughter?"

Aunt Cecelia stepped forward and offered her hand. The woman merely looked at it, so Aunt Cecelia dropped her arm. "My name is Cecelia, I am Morris West's aunt, and this here is Nandi and Patti. We're not sure if we are at the right address." Aunt Cecelia said with such eloquence.

"Why didn't y'all say that in the first place?" The lady laughed.

"Say what?" Aunt Cecelia asked.

"That you was kin to Chuck. Whenever anyone asks for Morris, we think they're from the government, wanting to get in our business." She stood back and opened the screen door wider. "Come on inside. Chuck went down to the store. He'll be back shortly."

"No, we'll wait in the car," Aunt Cecelia said, casting a glance in the

house.

"Oh, no. I can't let no kin to Chuck sit in the car when he's got chairs

in here," the lady said with a deep Southern accent.

Aunt Cecelia looked back at Patti and I and signaled for us to go in

with her.

Three cats followed us into the living room. The woman went in ahead of us and removed the stacks of magazines and clothes from the couch. She patted it with her hand as if to get all the dust particles out.

"Have a seat. By the way, my name is Sylvia. Can I get y'all anything to drink or eat?"

I panicked for a moment at the thought of consuming anything prepared in that filthy house.

Aunt Cecilia came to the rescue. "Oh, no. We're fine, thanks."

"Make yourselves at home, then." Sylvia pulled a box of cigarettes from her morning robe pocket. "I'll be right back. If you need me, I'll be out on the back porch."

The minute we heard the screen door slam, I leaned around Patti on the couch, where we sat like birds on a telephone line. "Aunt Cecelia, who is that lady?" I whisper shouted.

Aunt Cecelia looked around to make sure coast was clear. When she established we were safe to talk she whispered back. "Oh, child, I have no idea."

"We're in the heart of the ghetto," Patti whispered. "Do you think my car is safe out there?" Patti chuckled.

"Honey, I can only pray for it to be safe. Other than that, I couldn't tell you. This neighborhood gives me an uneasy feeling."

"This whole house gives me an uneasy feeling," I whispered back.

"What is that smell?"

"It must be a mixture of animal pee and all else that goes on in this house," Aunt Cecelia said, perched on the very edge of the couch.

"I know. This house is filthy!" Patti grimaced. "Do you think we're at the right house? She calls him Chuck, but you call him Morris."

Cecelia looked around again before talking and whispered. "I think

we are. I do remember that Lois used to call him Chuck."

Something black and ugly crawled by my foot which caused me to let out a little scream before I stomped on it.

"Eww! Was that a roach?" Patti asked, her face pinched as if it had

crawled across her lap rather than the floor.

"Calm down, ladies," Aunt Cecelia said, not moving a muscle.

I looked towards the screen and whispered. "It's disgusting in this house, and these cats are creeping me out. They keep purring and looking at us as if they want to devour us." Maybe coming here wasn't such a great idea. "Can we at least sit outside?"

"And get bit by a snake?" Patti shuddered. "There's no telling what

inhabits that long grass." We all couldn't help it but laugh at the situation.

Our conversation was cut short by a barking-coughing sound from the back porch. When it had persisted for a good thirty seconds, I stood and headed toward the back porch. Even though Sylvia was filthy, I couldn't let her choke out there. I poked my head outside.

"Are you okay? Can I get you some water?"

"I'm fine, hon." Sylvia snorted up some phlegm and spat-shot it out into the grass. Then she took a long drag from her long, unwashed cigarette. "You look like your father. Your nose, those eyes, and that complexion."

"Thank you." I said calmly while half distracted.

I turned and strode back into the living room, the woman's words still banging around in my brain. How could she say such a thing?

*   *   *

"I think that's Morris," Patti said, her voice betraying excitement that I didn't feel. I stood and paced the living room, biting my nails.

"That's just what your momma used to do when she was nervous." Aunt Cecelia scooted herself further to the edge of the couch, clasped her purse, and sat upright.

"What are they doing?" Patti asked as she continued to peek out the

window.

I crossed the small room in four strides. "Who?"

"Your dad and Sylvia." Patti moved the drape out of her way. "Oh,

never mind. They're walking this way now. She might have been telling him he has visitors or something."

Patti left the window and sat next to Aunt Cecelia. "Nandi!" "What?" I startled and spun toward her. "You scared me half to death." "Sit down." Patti said as the front door opened.

I sat on Aunt Cecelia's other side, all three of us gripped with silence. Then we heard footsteps, a strange halting gait that sounded like a wooden-legged pirate in the hallway. The steps stopped briefly at the doorway to the living room.

When Aunt Cecelia exhaled as though bracing herself, I leaned into her and grabbed her hand. A tall, skinny man, whose right leg told a story of amputation at the knee joint who was supported by crutches, stood in the doorway. He looked at me, then Aunt Cecelia, then Patti. He held a long can, its top visible over the brown bag it was in, and he lifted that bag and guzzled its contents.

Then he started toward the recliner opposite us. His crutches were missing their rubber grips, so every time the crutches hit the wooden floor, they made a thudding noise. At the chair, he used one crutch to shoo the cats away, and with the same swipe, he knocked aside the clothes that were strewn on it.

When he'd positioned himself on the recliner, he lay his brown bag

and its contents on the overly used lamp table. Sylvia came running in without her morning robe this time, wearing instead a pair of stained jeans and an oversized, wrinkled t-shirt. She had a cigarette and a lighter in her hand.

"This here is your kin."

"I know who she is!" His voice was deep and raspy and angry.

Sylvia turned around and headed for the back porch.

The living room filled with an uncomfortable silence. Finally, Aunt Cecelia broke it.

"Ladies, can you excuse Morris and me for a minute? Perhaps you can visit with Sylvia outside." I stood and left the room first. Then Patti followed, and we headed toward the back. Patti started to shut the door when Sylvia gave her a pointed look. "Leave that door open. The screen is enough."

Patti's eyes widened, but she did as the woman said. She looked around and then waved toward a bench positioned at the edge of a makeshift garden.

"Is it okay if we sit on that bench?" Patti asked.

Sylvia nodded, a cigarette hanging out the side of her mouth. By now, I felt as though we were invading enemy territory. Sylvia crushed her cigarette butt beneath her heel and then picked it up and threw it into an overflowing makeshift ashtray. Then she sat next to me on the bench. "What happened to my father's leg?" I asked.

"They amputated it, due to his diabetes. That was years ago before we met."

The sound of shouting inside the house interrupted her. I rushed to the door, where I could hear.

"You know she's your daughter." Aunt Cecelia's voice floated through the screen.

Morris's sarcastic laugh shot right through the screen door. "I don't

have no daughter. All I've ever had is a son."

"Stop right there. You know you have a daughter. When you came in, you admitted you knew who she was."

"Yeah, well." His loud, slurred tone made her imagine an ugly sneer on his face. "Who's to say she's mine?"

"Unbelievable." Aunt Cecelia's voice rose as loud as Morris's. "After all these years, you still deny her. I would have thought by now you would..." "Would what?"

This was beginning to sound dangerous. I turned to Sylvia. "I think we should go inside and check on Aunt Cecelia," readying myself to stand up for my aunt.

"I think you should let them talk. They're adults," Sylvia said.

"But..."

Sylvia grabbed my wrist and squeezed it hard. "Let them be, child."

I sat back down. For once, I wished I could pray. For my aunt, of

course. Not for myself.

"So, we understand that Nandi has an older brother?" Patti asked.

Sylvia touched her lighter to the tip of her cigarette, shielding the flame from the wind. She squinted one eye as she took a long drag from her cigarette. "You talking about MJ?" Sylvia said, exhaling smoke with her words.

Patti was waving her hand in front of her face as to deter the smoke

from her face. "Yes." Patti said.

Secretly I wished Patti and Sylvia would end the conversation because my eyes and ears were fixated on the hollering inside the house.

Sylvia laughed then had a coughing fit. She patted her chest, snorted through her nose, and spat some phlegm out on the grass. "His name is Morris Junior," Sylvia said around the cigarette hanging out of her mouth. "MJ has been in the pen for the last ten years that I've known

Morris Senior."

My brother in prison? Surely not. "Wait, Pen as in penitentiary?" I

asked.

"See there. You're not so high society as I thought you were. You know some street lingo." Sylvia laughed and took a drag.

"Yes. Pen, like the penitentiary."

Something in me had to know what my brother did. "If you don't

mind me asking..."

"He murdered someone." Sylvia chuckled.

What was wrong with this woman? "Murder is not funny."

I insisted.

"I know it's not. I'm laughing at the look on your face."

Could this situation get any worse? "What do you mean he murdered

someone? Who? I mean how? Why..."

Sylvia held up one hand. "Let me stop you right there before you lose your mind. I wasn't there, but word on the street says it was a drunken driving accident. MJ was high and drunk, traveling on one of them back roads, when he lost control and went head-on with a family in a minivan. I heard that the impact of his truck sent that minivan spiraling down the embankment and only the father survived."

"Are you serious?" Patti interrupted Sylvia.

"Serious as a heart attack. He's in the pen for three life terms. The momma in that car died on the spot. The two young children, ages seven and three, were airlifted to the nearest hospital and lost their lives that night. I heard that your dad liked to drink back in the day, but after this, all went down, he stayed drunk."

"No, it can't be…" Nothing going on in that house could be as bad as what I was hearing out here. I moved back to the door and listened in again, hearing Aunt Cecelia's voice.

"I thought by now you would have come to terms with life and could

acknowledge the other child you created with…"

"With who? Have you come here today to badger me about the mistake I made years and years ago?" Morris slurred.

"Mistake!" Aunt Cecelia hollered. "I don't even know why we came

here. Some things never change."

"Did you think I was going to be excited to see you, of all people, here in my house today?"

Aunt Cecelia heaved a huge sigh. The couch creaked as if she was standing up. "That's right. Leave."

In the silence that followed Morris's rude comment, I imagined my aunt's shocked, hurt expression. Then footsteps sounded again as if she was moving closer to him again. "How do you think your uncle would feel, knowing you're talking to me like this?"

"The greedy old man is dead, so I don't care what he would think."

"You are a shame and a disgrace to your family. How dare you call your late uncle greedy after all he did for you?" Cecelia's voice lost all its previous gentleness. "We bent over backward for you. All you did was take everything we gave you and waste it. You betrayed your own flesh and blood in the worst way ever. You've stolen from us, lied to us, and guess who still stood by your side? Your greedy uncle and I when your own momma disowned you. Unbelievable! You need deliverance."

At the sound of her footsteps nearing the door, I scrambled away, so my aunt wouldn't see me eavesdropping.

A moment later, Aunt Cecelia stormed out of the house.

"Ladies! Let's get going."

As we said our goodbyes to Sylvia, Morris stumbled into the yard and propped himself against the doorframe. "You know I was supposed to get that money and land. Unk C. left some of that to me," he slurred.

Cecelia acted as though she did not hear him. The more she ignored him, the more pugnacious he became. We started toward Aunt Cecelia, ready to leave. Morris moved quicker than I would have thought possible, in his condition, and blocked the walkway to the car. Aunt Cecelia grabbed my hand, and I grabbed Patti's hand, and together we plunged right into the muddy yard at the edge of the walk. Morris continued hollering, following us to the car.

"Nandi, Patti, get in. I will be right with you." Cecelia said in a calm

tone as she stood in a mud puddle by the rock driveway.

"Come on. Let's just go," I pleaded.

"We will, baby, in a second. I have one more thing to do." She stood to her full height and looked Morris in the eye. "What are you so angry about?"

"I'm not angry. You the one who was yelling at me and calling me all kinds of names."

"I am not arguing with a drunk. You need help!"

"I don't need help. I just want my fair share of my uncle's money."

"Your uncle never owed you anything. You failed to meet the conditions under which you would receive an inheritance from him. Therefore, you get nothing from your uncle or me." Aunt Cecelia turned her back to him, opened the car door, and got in. "Let's get out of here."

Patti placed the car in reverse and drove us out of Alabama without one of us turning our heads back. After a time of silence,

Aunt Cecelia finally spoke. "I'm sorry you two had to see him in that condition. That was why I was so reluctant to bring you here. Are you okay, Nandi?" I nodded but couldn't bring myself to speak or look at my aunt during the entire ride.

CHAPTER SIXTEEN

Mississippi 2014

We arrived at Cecelia's home, I still couldn't manage to speak. I grabbed my purse and headed upstairs to my room, leaving Patti and Cecelia to say what they would about me. "Do you think Nandi overheard her father and me?" Aunt Cecelia's voice traveled up the staircase.

I slammed the door, not wanting to hear more. I packed my bags and then I laid on the bed, unable to stop my tears. I needed to get out of here. And I needed answers. Why did I even come with Patti, to begin with?

The door opened, and my aunt and Patti walked in. Aunt Cecelia sat beside me and placed her hand on my shoulder.

"I don't understand. I want the truth." I demanded.

Aunt Cecelia sighed. "Where do you want me to start?"

"With Momma Jean's marriage to that man. With my brother. Why did Morris disown me? Is he really my father?" Even though the conversation was between Aunt Cecelia and Morris I can't help but feel really hurt by some of the things Morris was saying. I feel as though I have hit a brick wall and this road trip was a waste of time.

"I don't want to hurt you any more than you already are." Cecelia said with compassion.

Ha! I huffed. "It's too late. The damage was done long ago."

"Then let's start with your late great-uncle Charlie since you want to know everything. It's your right to know the absolute truth about your family. I believe that, through God's help, you can rewrite the direction of your bloodline."

Aunt Cecelia rubbed my back, just as Momma Jean used to.

"When I met your great uncle, he loved to drink, just like your pappy. After he was saved he gave his testimony in church. After that, he made it his business to help Lois and her son, your father, to find salvation in Christ." Cecelia exhaled and softly spoke. "Years came and went, and finally Lois was saved. She took your father to church every Sunday and to weekday services. She was fired up for God, but Charlie and I knew that something within her hadn't been healed. She needed deliverance. This is not judgment. It's discernment." I couldn't but help the look Cecelia had on her face.

Her mouth was slightly frowned and her eyebrows slightly drooped. She reminded me of a mourner at a funeral. I could tell that she was bothered by what she was saying. All this time she had been here for me and it was now my time to sit back and listen.

"Charlie and I spent years fasting and praying for her and believing God for her breakthrough. Some event in her childhood must have turned her into an angry person. She took out her rage on your father. Back then, there was no Child Protective Services where Lois lived." Cecelia stopped talking abruptly and then I heard a gasp.

"Morris spent his summers with us, just to get away from his mother. We spent many visits talking to Lois, but she never wanted to listen. Later, she cut us off from seeing Morris. Charlie and I did all we could to see Morris, but because we were not his parents, we couldn't take her to court." Cecelia's voice cracked, I could feel her hand shaking on my back as she rubbed my back.

"We had no way to prove she was an abusive, unfit mother. So, we kept our distance. We were hurt but we continued to pray and fast for Lois. When Morris turned eighteen, he married Morris Junior's mother. At that time, we reconnected with Morris without Lois's permission. Everything was great." In all this, I couldn't help but feel sorry for my aunt.

"We loved Morris's first wife and he was proving himself to being a good father. Charlie hired him to work in one of our businesses, as Charlie and I prepared to move up North. Morris accepted the position and worked tirelessly helping Charlie and me. We were proud of him." Cecelia let out a delighted laugh. "You would never believe me if I told you that your pappy was the best organist in all of Mississippi, at least the church and I thought so. He also helped Charlie and I start our church. Life was good until his wife died while giving birth to their second child." Cecelia looked up towards the ceiling with her mouth sucked in she took in a deep breath through her nose. Then she blurted out.

"Then the baby died a few days later. All of that was too hard for Morris to comprehend. Charlie and I did our best to support and counsel him, but he was devastated. Stella was his high school sweetheart, the only woman he ever loved. Morris raised Morris Junior with the help of his mother. Years later, your mother started visiting our church."

"Oh. Wow." I said. What else could I add to that my heart was broken from Momma's passing and to imagine my father lost his wife and child made me feel kind of sorry for him.

"Shortly before your mammy became a member, her great-grand mammy passed away. It was too hard for Jean to remain a part of the church she'd attended with her great-grand mammy. So, she decided to find another home church, one without the memories of her loss, and she came to our church. We were conveniently located, close to the university she was attending." Cecelia broke out a proud chuckle before continuing to talk…. "Your momma loved to sing, and she was blessed with a beautiful singing voice. We had only two choir members, as we had just pioneered the church. When your momma joined our church, she coached everyone who had a desire to sing. Before long, she had a decent choir." Cecelia couldn't hold back her contagious giggle.

"As she worked alongside the musicians, she caught Morris's attention. Soon they started courting. They got married, and one year after the wedding, your momma gave birth to a beautiful baby girl, whom she named Nandi. Your pappy wanted to name you Melissa, but Jean was headstrong about naming you Nandi." Cecelia chuckled. "You were a happy family at first." Cecelia's tone quickly turned sober.

"What happened?" I asked.

"We had no idea where your parent's marriage went wrong or how long things had been an array. I felt bad that I was not intuitive enough to recognize how rocky the marriage had become. When your momma finally had enough, she came to Charlie and me for counseling. We had a hard time believing that Morris would treat your momma as she said he did." Cecelia lowered her tone. "Charlie and I did what any other loving relative would do, or so we thought. We encouraged her to stay with her husband. We didn't know the severity of the situation in her home, because whenever we saw Morris, he seemed like the same Morris Charlie and I always knew, happy-go-lucky." Cecelia removed her hand away from my back and folded her arms on her chest.

"We did finally confront him about his marriage, but he denied the allegations. He fooled me, he fooled Charlie, and, for the longest time, he fooled his own momma. I guess when he returned home from work, he drowned himself in alcohol. Then he barraged your momma with hurtful and mean words."

I hate to admit it, but it was making a lot more sense to me at that point. I was beginning to understand why Momma didn't want to mention him. "I don't know how long he had been self-medicating with alcohol, but I felt horrible for not believing your momma initially. By the time Charlie and I intervened, we had found out that he had stolen substantial amounts of money from our businesses." I sat up straight thrown back by what Cecelia was saying.

My father was not only an alcoholic, but he was a thief too! I didn't know how to digest it all. I mean one part of me was happy knowing I didn't grow up in such a home but the other part of me was dwelling on the fact that this man's blood runs deep in my veins.

"That's when we realized he was not the same Morris we'd known when he was a boy. Your momma left Morris, and Lois took you both in. Morris had run off to Alabama to preach, from what we heard. Lois' home was convenient for your momma because it was close to the university she was attending."

"To Preach? A thief and alcoholic?" I was aggravated by this news. I don't understand.

Cecelia forced a laugh. "Oh-child! I highly doubted if that's what really happened. Lois allegedly stated that that's what he did but knowing Lois, she said it to make him look good like she didn't know that Charlie and I knew of his drinking and thieving ways!" Cecelia released her hands from her chest and laid them on her laps with her fingers laced together.

"Charlie and I wanted to take you both North with us, but Momma Jean had a full scholarship, and Lois promised to take good care of you two. I had no choice but to believe Lois since she was your biological grandmother." Cecelia paused and sighed as she gazed out the window.

"What did Morris mean when he said I wasn't his daughter?" A part of me wanted to know but, not really because I felt like that was mean of him to have said.

"Oh, honey. Your father is slowly but surely losing it, and we need to pray for him." Aunt Cecelia's tone sounded soft and confident. "You're his daughter." She affirmed her response with a stern headshake.

"Then why would he say that?"

Cecelia removed her glasses and tilted her head down as if in shame.

"I have no explanation. That's a deep-seated issue from his days in his mother's hands. Lois never claimed him as her son until later in life, and when he became a full-fledged drunk and removed himself from the church, Lois stopped claiming him once again." Cecelia's voice sounded sad.

"We didn't know that she abused him, physically and mentally, until years later. Stella was the only person your father felt safe with. Then she passed away, and he never recovered from the loss. He might even have retreated back into his memories of growing up in

Lois's house, judging from some of the things Jean mentioned to Charlie and me."

All this time I faulted Momma for not talking to me about my father and only to realize given the circumstances, I wouldn't want to talk about him too. "Your momma was strong enough to put up with your father all those years. She did not intend to hurt you when she kept you from your biological father. Your momma faced a lot, and knowing Jean, she must have thought she was protecting you. But parents can make mistakes, and all I can say is that it would be wrong for you to hold a grudge or resentment toward your late mother. She did all she knew to do...."

"I don't understand why she didn't tell me the whole truth."

Cecelia sighed. "Baby that is easier said than done. The good Lord knows that the truth can be hard to handle or even speak of. Let me ask you this: would you have believed your momma if she'd told you your biological father was an abusive drunk and that she left him to give you a better life?"

"No! I wouldn't have."

Cecelia shrugged her shoulders and raised one eyebrow. "Then I hope you understand why your momma shielded you from him in the first place. The pain you're feeling right now is exactly what your loving mother didn't want you to experience."

"It's okay for her to decide whether my biological father is important in my lif—?"

"I never said that. But I did say that you cannot get angry about your late mother's actions. You also can't get mad at your father. You wanted to meet him, so you met him. I, of all people, would have loved for it to be under different circumstances. But your fairy tale does not end like that. This is as real as life gets." Cecelia stood up and walked towards the window.

"Morris is still my nephew, whether through marriage or not. He is my kin and I love him dearly. All I can do for him now is pray for him, pray that the strongman of alcoholism will leave him while he can still repent. All I have is you. I have lived long enough to see what the bondage of alcohol has done to your family." Cecelia went into a daze

with her eyes fixated passed the window.

"By all goodness, Nandi, I am counting on you to be the generational curse stopper, the one who declares an end to this curse and bind it for good." Cecelia said in a monotone voice.

"What do you mean curse?"

"Hand me that Bible on the nightstand." I reached for the Bible and stood up to walk towards Cecelia, she leafed through the pages and then, presumably finding the spot she wanted, she shut the Bible with her index finger holding her place.

"Before I get into generational curses, I want to ask you a few personal questions. Understand I am not here to judge you, mock you, or make fun of you. Since you've been here, I merely felt in my spirit that you are troubled, and God has revealed a couple of things to me. I want to help you the best way I know how. Is that okay?"

CHAPTER SEVENTEEN

Provenance

"Wat kind of relationship did you have with Lois?" Cecelia asked.

That was the last thing I had expected my aunt to say. But as much as I didn't want to revisit those days, I had an odd feeling that I needed to before I could be healed. I breathed a prayer for help, a surprise in itself.

"What relationship? I had a relationship with her leather belts, shoes, and iron cords. Not with her."

Cecelia sat down by the bay window. "Okay, you had a relationship

with her belts. I get that. How did she treat you? And how did that make you feel?"

I don't know why I get agitated when I talk about Lois. "Oh, no. I

know where this is going. At first, I thought I could talk about it, but now I don't know. I've already told all those therapists and counselors about it."

Cecelia had her index finger lining on her chin like she was getting

ready to get her picture taken.

"About what? What are you so afraid of talking about?"

Ugh. So annoying. "I am not afraid of anything. It's just that..."

Cecelia drew a cold stare on me that made me feel weird.

"It's just that what? Child, what hurt you so badly that you now bend forward in defeat like this?"

"What are you talking about?"

Cecelia sighed. "I could smell your hurt from a mile away. I could

sense your pain since you arrived here."

"Now you know me? You know my whole life history. Is this what you and Patti have been up to?" Cecelia drew closer. "Aunt Cecelia don't need to talk to nobody to know that something is troubling you. Now, if you quit being so defensive, I might be able to help you. I can guide you and perhaps counsel you so you won't waste the rest of your life, living on yesterday's hurts and pains."

My heart broke at my Auntie's stern words. My tears fell afresh.

"Nobody other than Brian and Momma has ever genuinely cared for me like you have done these last couple of days."

"That is why you can talk to me. Let me help you." Aunt Cecelia stood up from the bay window and walked towards the bed to sit closer to me.

"I don't know if anyone can help me anymore. My whole life is a mess. I don't even know how and when I got here, but I am here.

I might not have a husband when I get home. I have no idea what I'm going to do with my life." The sober reality of my mess hurt me deeper than I could ever imagine because for years I hadn't allowed myself to feel.

Aunt Cecelia turned towards me and used the back of her hand to wipe my tears away. "Don't speak like that. You'll have a husband when you get home. That man loves you enough to have stayed around this long. He ain't–sure–gonna leave you when you get back." The confidence in her tone gave me a little hope. But not enough to speak out.

My journey in life started at the home Momma Jean and I shared with Lois. She beat me for everything I did or tried to do. She called me all kinds of awful names. Many times, I wanted to tell Momma when she got home, but I thought Momma wouldn't believe me because, after all, I was just a little child. I can still see Lois' face today, filled with so much hate for me.

When we arrived in East St. Louis, all Momma did was work and go to school. I thought she didn't like being at home with me, and that was why she stayed away. But when I got older, I realized she had to put food on our table and keep a roof over our head, and that her absence was not her way of staying away.

I got that. But even when I was older, Momma Jean and I never connected. On rare occasions, she told me she loved me. Those times were so rare that I never knew what affection or real love was. When I was thirteen years old, a neighborhood boy named Frank molested me. Initially, I didn't know what it all meant. One day, he and his sister gave me a ride home from school.

I had been waiting for the rain to pass. After that, I thought I could trust him. I knew something was awkward when he started coming to school just to pick me up, and not his sister.

At first, I believed his lies of concern, until one day when he drove me to an abandoned field. He parked the car and forced me to put my hand in his pants. I was terrified because he told me he would kill me and Momma Jean if I told her. I believed him because he had spent time in jail. For the next several months, he picked me up every day and drove me to the field and put his hands up my skirt.

I didn't know what to do, and I didn't know who to tell. I was so glad when he was locked up for good. I finally felt safe. If I'd told momma what happened to me, she would have deemed me unholy. She would have blamed me for everything since I was not supposed to accept rides from anyone.

"I understand if you despise talking about Lois. But understand that we naturally tend to make certain decisions based on our past. Since Lois often told you negative things about yourself, then you probably began to live that reality. Not purposely, but unconsciously. I am not placing blame on anyone in specific but on the words released into your life at such an innocent age," Aunt Cecelia said as she placed her reading glasses back on her face.

I still was uncertain about how much to tell. "As far as Lois is concerned, I have memories of horrible events that I don't feel comfortable talking about. These memories are of events that happened from the time I was five years old all the way up to my tenth birthday." It was hard for me to articulate the verbal and physical abuse without feeling as though I was going to lose my mind.

"Excuse me one second." I said. I had to go to the bathroom for some type of space. I raced into the bathroom and closed and locked the door. I had an emotional outburst in which I could not control. I slid down the wall until I was sitting on the floor, my knees against my chest I tried rocking myself back and forth to calm myself but that didn't help.

"Listen to me, Nandi. It's going to be okay, you hear? Open the door, honey," Aunt Cecelia hollered, rattling the doorknob.

Over the sound of my own voice, I heard Patti demanding to know what was going on.

"She locked herself in the bathroom, and she won't come out," Aunt Cecelia said with a wavering voice to Patti.

"Let me try," Patti said. "Nandi, open up right now!" The doorknob rattled again, over and over.

"No! Why … why? Oh, God, why?" I hollered through my tears.

The banging and rattling finally stopped. Then the door flung open, and Patti stood there, apparently having picked the lock with a quarter as she always had when we used to lock ourselves out of the dorm. Patti walked into the bathroom and sat on the edge of the tub, close enough to me to rub my back. Aunt Cecelia shut the toilet lid and sat on it and grabbed my hand.

"What has got you so upset?" Aunt Cecelia asked.

"It's like she never cared." I felt a thin sense of unreality take over my mind. "When she looked at me in the hospital, she was just cold and stoic. I was sure that, deep down, she blamed me for the rape, both mine and Clara's."

"Who never cared?" Aunt Cecelia asked.

"Momma. I lay on that cold hospital bed in shock, in physical pain, but she never once came close to me to embrace me or empathize with me." I still remember it like it was yesterday, she just stood there in silence. When we left the hospital, she never once talked about it.

I knew I had let her down in the worst way possible, although all I ever wanted was to make her proud of me. But the more I tried, the more I failed. I didn't want to be a medical doctor, but I felt bad that she had spent most of her life's savings for me to attend college and medical school, so I went. Even after that, I still let her down.

The only person I thought I had was Clara, until the accident. Momma never liked Clara and Brian never cared for her either, but I felt as though she was one of the few who cared for me. Little did I know then that she was all about her own selfish agendas.

I should've known she was not a true friend when she chose not to testify against the DJ who raped us. All I ever wanted was a mother who loved me and taught me about life and wouldn't judge me for my flaws or think I was a heathen each and every time I fell. I just wanted her to reach her hand out and guide me through life and tell me that she would love me no matter what career path I chose or no matter what I did. I have felt like a complete loser most of my life.

Lois never cared for me, Momma could be bothered less by me, and the boys never really cared for me either. Lord knows I had reached my wits end in college when I was dogged out by a boy for the umpteenth time. I couldn't do it to myself anymore. I had no God. I spent many months in depression. I tried killing myself multiple times but failed. The only thing that could help me cope was alcohol. When I took a shot or a sip of alcohol, it always radiated to my spine first, and my head became instantly light and free of care. I didn't experience so many nightmares, and I didn't want to kill myself anymore because all I wanted to do was drink. I just wanted Momma to be proud of me and to act like she loved me.

Cecelia opened her Bible to the page that her index finger had been holding in place. "You have experienced a lot in your life, and the only way it can get better from here is to understand that God loves you. He sent His son to die for you and me, paying our sins in full. John 8:36 says that if the Son sets you free, you will be free indeed. Do you believe Jesus is able to set you free from all your hurt, pain, disappointment, depression and bondage?" Aunt Cecelia continued to flip through her Bible.

"I guess ..."

"And it also says here in Romans 10:9-10, 'Because, if you confess with your mouth that Jesus is Lord and believe in your heart that God raised him from the dead, you will be saved. For with the heart one believes and is justified, and with the mouth, one confesses and is saved.' Do you believe that, Nandi?" Cecelia asked.

I nodded my head, barely able to find my voice. "Something has to give. I can't live like this anymore. I want something new, and I believe it, Aunt Cecelia. I believe Jesus can help me!"

"Amen!" Cecelia hollered. Then she laid her hands on my shoulders and prayed for me.

"I will take you to my special friend Billie tomorrow," Auntie said when she finished her prayer. "She has a ministry based upon deliverance, and there I will tell you more about generational curses, now that we have had this talk."

EPILOGUE

A Year Later

Never in my life had I imagined a life so complete, a life so happy and peaceful. Aunt Cecelia was the best birthday present I'd ever had in my life.

Three weeks after Patti and I left Aunt Cecelia's in Mississippi, my aunt passed away. Her abdominal aneurysm ruptured while she was asleep. The news was sad but as a new believer in Christ, I was at peace,

knowing she had gone on to be with the Lord. It was unfortunate that Brian never got a chance to meet her, but she left me the most valuable gift of living afresh in Christ. For that I thank God.

Before Patti and I left Mississippi, Aunt Cecelia introduced me to

Billie. She and I have had a great spiritual relationship. Billie helped deliver me after I surrendered my life to Christ, and God has taken away any desire for alcohol from my mind and tongue. I can't believe that after all the professional help Brian got me, the only step

I needed was one big step toward God. And I finally accepted the fact that I was an alcoholic.

Aunt Cecelia had been right. I was in spiritual warfare. Especially
when it came down to my bloodline. Aunt Cecelia loved to recite Ephesians 6:12 and Lamentations 5:7 I started to think those were her two favorite Scriptures, but now I understand that she was preparing me for freedom from the sins of my forefathers and foremothers.

She wanted me to be ready to fight spiritually for the bloodline that
uncle Charlie died fighting for. This made sense to me since Lois West's father died as an alcoholic, my own father was an alcoholic, and Uncle Charlie was too before he came to Christ. Morris Junior my half-brother, was an alcoholic and then I was an alcoholic.

When Aunt Cecelia explained generational curses and familiar spirits, I couldn't do anything but awaken to a whole new level of truth. I knew if I kept going and drowning myself in alcohol, I would be bound for good. Then I could easily end up in jail or worse, dead. I am grateful that Aunt Cecelia helped to open my eyes to the truth after I told her of my life's hurts and pains. No one wants to face the fact that they have lost their way and now they depend on substances to help them cope. But the more we try to deny life's hurts, pains, and disappointments, the more the seed germinates and could possibly turn into an oversized weed of bondage.

That's what happened to me. All my life, I watched Momma cry in prayer. I watched her praise God as though she had lost her mind, but today, as a saved and delivered Christian, I understand why Momma was that way. God's love is so comforting, and His unconditional love despite my flaws makes me fall in love with Him which has also taught me to love my husband.

Salvation is a journey, not an overnight haul. I am learning to enjoy every step of the way. Aunt Cecelia gave me her Bible before we left Mississippi, and I read it every day. When I returned home, I was baptized in water. Shortly after that, at our church revival, I was baptized in the Spirit. I never saw the direction my life was going, but God knew. Shortly after Aunt Cecelia passed away, her lawyer traveled to St. Louis to meet with Brian and me.

Surprisingly enough, she willed to me all her estate, including over two million dollars. Brian and I were caught off guard by her generosity, and I knew then why the Lord had laid a great vision on my heart without releasing the source of the finances. I was able to start an addictions ministry that deals with divine intervention and deliverance. I have partnered with Billie to accomplish the work at hand.

Patti and I are as close as ever, and I frequently assist her and Pierre with their ministry. Brian and I paid off all our debtors, and Brian built us our dream home west of St. Louis, in the valley. He hired more employees for our architectural business.

The highlight of our marriage was when we renewed our vows. Shortly after that, I found out I was pregnant. Just the other day, we found out it's a boy. We have agreed to call him Isaac. His middle name will be Charles, after uncle Charlie.

One of the greatest lessons Aunt Cecelia taught me was the power of forgiveness. When I realized that I had to forgive myself first for all that has happened to me, I felt an enormous weight lifting off my shoulders. Then Aunt Cecelia walked me by forgiving others. I forgave my late mother for using all her past hurts and pains to support a lie. I also forgave her for shielding me from my biological father. I forgave Clara. Though I didn't realize it, I blamed her, not myself for my alcoholism, for messing up my medical career. That was a big revelation.

I forgave all the guys who had broken my heart. I forgave Mr. Kenny for walking out on me and Momma. I forgave those who violated me, molested me, and raped me. I forgave Lois West for the pain and hurt she inflicted. Above all, I forgave my biological father for disowning me and for what he did to my mother even before I knew him or knew it. I forgave my father for his ways. I forgave him for never desiring a relationship with me.

Shortly after all this forgiving, my father came looking for me. He had nothing but the clothes on his back. His longtime girlfriend, Sylvia, had left him. He had nothing, no money, no shelter, no food. So, Brian and I took him in. Taking care of him was the least I could do for my biological father. He has become our latest deliverance project, though he still struggles with his addiction. We stand united in my home in prayer over his soul. I will not allow the devil to claim his soul.

THE END

Dear Beloved,

What a journey. I was in tears in some parts, I smiled in others. I was disappointed in some parts and happy and relieved in others. I thank God for the great blessing of revelation. Like you, I was surprised with every chapter. I believe in the Holy Spirit's guidance which, made every chapter a beautiful surprise. This book took me on an incredibly emotional ride. I learned some amazing truths, which I would like to share.

Nandi allowed me to look at my own life and re-evaluate some missing links from the chain of my life's journey. I was saved some years ago. Before my salvation, I had always been in church, but for family reasons. Church was simply what my family did on Sundays. Growing up, I never had my own personal relationship with Christ. So, when I moved out on my own at age twenty-two, I stopped attending church.

After being absent from church for years, I came back to the one source I knew; Jesus. Once I was saved, I eventually received water baptism. Then I received the baptism of the Holy Spirit. It was an amazing feeling, and most of my experience with Holy Spirit baptism is detailed in my memoir, Born Again Afresh: How Struggling Christians Can Get Back on Track. It was wonderful to know that I now had a personal relationship with God through Jesus.

But although I was hungry and saved, I fought an inner battle. After salvation, I thought in my naive mind and from what I saw among some "Christians" that strength was what Christians were all about. So,

with that ignorance, I walked around thinking I had victory over my past. Little did I know, I was in denial of my past. Nandi helped me understand how crippling denial can be. Denial is the first cousin of deceit, so small wonder that I still struggled with an addiction.

Like Nandi, I was an alcoholic for nine years. But even during the

darkest and loneliest moments, I still believed God would eventually redeem me and deliver me of my addiction. Nandi and I have totally different backgrounds, but we share a common aspect of addiction. My denial process began when I was thirteen. A group of boys sexually violated me. Naïve and not understanding, I tried to move on with my life. I didn't know that something really bad had just happened to me, and I chose not to think about it. In one sense, I repressed any memory of it.

When I was fourteen, the cousin of a close friend sexually violated me. I was still naïve and now confused. Once again, I chose to deny it. What made it worse this time was that, when I told my close friend what her cousin did, she did not believe me. That taught me not to tell anyone anything. Sometimes the truth is hard to hide, but through the pain, I tried to conceal it and act normal.

That worked until the age of fifteen when I was raped. It was hard to accept the fact that my innocence had been taken. I wanted to be a virgin when I got married. I denied all the sexual violations.

In denying them, I carried a seed of denial and repressed horrible memories that would eventually grow and eat me alive.

From the age of fifteen to about seventeen, I had suicidal tendencies. After being raped, I wanted to take my own life because as much as I was in denial, I felt deep down inside that I would never be the same. I

hated myself and wanted out of this world. My many attempts at suicide failed, thank God. When I was eighteen, I was in a toxic relationship, one that was filled with mental and physical abuse. That was when I also discovered the numbing effects of alcohol. His abuse didn't bother me as long as I was drunk, then I couldn't feel anything, physically or emotionally. That relationship finally ended, but as the seed of denial grew, so did the deception.

For years, I felt insecure, due to years of hearing I was fat, ugly, and that no one would ever want me. I lived a life of hate, both self-hate and people-hate. My repressed-memories box opened wide and led to much more self-destructive behavior. Then came my salvation. I realized I had not confronted my past, and because of that, the door was still open. The more I tried not to think about it, the more it germinated in my mind.

I couldn't look my past in the eye since I was sober. Instead, I simply denied all the events that had transpired. I drank those memories away (temporarily). This caused the door of denial to open further and the thoughts of deception to occur. Therefore, even early in my salvation, I still struggled with alcoholism.

Only when I was completely delivered did God take the desire for alcohol away from my tongue, my mind, and my life. In the nine years of bondage, I had done everything I could think of to overcome alcoholism. (That is, I did the humanly possible, not the spiritually possible.) I checked myself into an outpatient rehabilitation center, only to relapse multiple times. My drinking became worse. My life was heading in a deep, downward spiral because of the seed of denial.

I understand that the good word (Bible) tells us to press for the prize of the high calling in Christ Jesus (Philippians 3:14). I also understand that some saints have used this Scripture as a buffer, acting strong and denying the past. They then ignore the deep issues of the past that affect them today in their walk.

I am not asking you to dwell in the past or to subject yourself to past pain, misery, and pity. But like Nandi, some things in our present behavior are a direct reflection of our past. And like Nandi, we can return to the source and origin of our pain. Then we can start to heal.

In returning to the source, I am not asking you to seek answers or

solutions. Rather, the source serves as a gateway of closure. I am free today and speak freely of my past pain and hurts because I confronted my past. I am no longer in denial of what happened to me. Instead, I live free in all truths, and the truth has set me free.

Perhaps you don't face alcohol abuse today. Maybe your struggle is with nicotine, pills, marijuana (weed), sex, pornography, gambling, adultery, prostitution, hoarding, food abuse, insecurity, jealousy, malice, manipulation, drugs, or something else. Many things can hinder us from a complete deliverance and closeness with God. Like Patti's mother, you might have a painstaking secret that you've hidden in your heart and denied to your children.

Maybe you have been married multiple times, and it's never your fault but always the other people. Perhaps you've denied the issues lying dominant in your life, and they keep you in a search for the next best thing. Maybe you have been in numerous tumultuous relationships, so you don't feel you deserve marriage or a man who can love you like Christ loved the church. And that has made you "Miss Independent."

Yet you secretly cry yourself to sleep at night, wondering what is going on with you and why no one will pay you any attention. You might have chosen to marry the wrong person or for the wrong reasons, so that marriage didn't last. Deep down inside, you hold bitter resentment for a man you knew was never interested in you. After you purposely trapped him by having children with him, you deny your involvement and blame everything on him. You tell the children he is a deadbeat, and yet you are just as liable. Your denial and lack of accountability are turning your
life to deception.

Maybe you have made crucial mistakes in life but deny them. (I am a woman too. I have been there, done that, passed that.) Maybe you experienced trauma, heartache, pain, or hurtful situations in your past, and they hold you in denial of your past and cripple your deliverance process and closeness with God. Hear me out, ladies! Never dwell in

your past. Never live in your past. Never create pity for your past.

Through my efforts and through Nandi's life, I learned it is crucial to understand the missing link in our connection with God. I realized before my deliverance that I did not want to confront my past. I wanted to be healed and saved and never think about my past, but the more I tried not to think about my past, the more I abused alcohol. I had never talked to anyone about these events in my life, let alone talk to myself about it. It was easier to deny the events, but that drove me to the edge of drowning all my emotions in alcohol.

I have lived here in the Midwest for some years now. The winters are no joke, compared to Southern California and Zimbabwe, where I was born. Some people take great pains to place plastic around the inside of the windows of their houses, or they buy devices that close up all the cracks, so the cold air won't seep in through them. The living room won't get warm in the winter if the front door is cracked open. You must physically walk to the front door and shut it if you want a warm house.

Likewise, as long as you are in denial of your past, you have a cracked

door to your past. You cannot expect to walk in full victory from your past if your door is cracked open. The pastor cannot shut the door to your past. Neither can his wife, the choir, or the church members. You should get up and physically shut the door to your own past.

You may believe you are over your past. You might be a strong Christian woman, blessed and highly favored, walking in victory with the Lord. Well, like you, I thought my door was shut. I too thought I walked in a victory over my past. But I surely wasn't walking in victory with a door cracked open while I battled alcoholism. You can deceive yourself into thinking the room is getting warmer while the winter draft seeps through the door crack. But you're the only one who will believe that. Your guests won't. Likewise, you can convince yourself that you walk in victory over your past, but you're the only person being deceived. Be mindful because as denial is a first cousin to deceit, bondage is the mother of deceit.

I realized my door to my past was not shut because I couldn't talk freely

about it. We don't want to boast about the past, but we do need to be able to talk about all our events. John 8:36 says, "So if the Son sets you free,

you will be free indeed." Without a doubt, I had surrendered my life to Christ, but I was not free. Deliverance had to happen first. I couldn't talk about the sexual, mental, and physical abuse, the alcoholism, or all the other childhood issues I experienced.

I thought if I kept them locked deep in the back of my head, I was over them. But I was not over them. You don't have to discuss all your past with anyone, but you do need to discuss it with God.

Sometimes, in order to leap from denial to reality, you must physically go to the source of your hurt, pain, rejection, and abuse. Then confront them to fulfill closure. You must be a victim before you are a victor, and the only way you can be a victor is by confrontation.

You can say, "This happened to me, but I forgive the people who caused my pain. I also forgive myself for holding onto it. From now on, I walk in Christ as a victor, not the victim. I now slam shut the door to my past.
I lock it and throw away the key."

In some cases, we need to seek Christian help from a close friend
and/or counsel from leadership in the church. We must choose our counselors wisely, praying and seeking God's direction and discernment. I shared my story with you because I no longer live in my past. In fact, I live far from my past in true strength as a victor and not a pity-seeker.

God's work is only starting in you. His deliverance process will restore
you. Remember to confront your past, because sweeping things under the rug will only cause a mound of obstacles later. Confront your past through forgiveness of self and others. Close the door and move forward.

I am now more deeply freed than I ever would have imagined. I thank God for the blessing and pray that you too are blessed and freed.

"So if the Son sets you free, you will be free indeed."

–John 8:36 ESV

"Saying to the prisoners, 'Come out,' to those who are in darkness, 'Appear.' They shall feed along the ways; on all bare heights shall be their pasture."*– Isaiah 49:9 ESV*

Then they cried to the Lord in their trouble, and he delivered them from their distress.

–Psalm 107:6 ESV

Group Discussion

Please share your answers at your own discretion, with discernment.

Was there a time in your life when you felt the following seeds;

- seeds of insecurity
- seeds of forgiveness
- seeds of doubt
- seeds of abandonment
- seeds of loneliness
- seeds of anxiety
- seeds of depression and or self-worthlessness?
- Unresolved issues with spouse,
- friends, and/or family.
- Negative seeds implanted in you in your childhood by a family member or friend.
- A feeling of disconnection from your family and/or friends.
- A major disappointment.
- Doubt/self-doubt.
- Denial (what was the truth?)
- justification that overshadowed the truth.
- Resentment toward a situation or person.
- How did the resentment start?

- o Friends whom your family considered a bad influence. How did you handle it?
- o Hurt, pain, trauma, and tragedy. What have they taught you?
- o A friend or family member misusing your trust.
- o Betrayal. How did it make you feel?

Please share with the group how you overcame these seeds, how you felt before overcoming, and how you felt after overcoming. Also, please discuss the possibility of never overcoming.

Insecurity. On a scale of 1-10, with 10 being very secure and 1 being very insecure, how do you rate your own security? Why?

If you could give someone in your group today a word of non-judgmental encouragement, what would it be, and why?

Author's Commentary

I confronted the events of my childhood. It wasn't easy because, for years, I feared them and ran from them by drinking myself to sleep. But because of my relationship with Jesus Christ, I can be honest with myself. I can look at my life and understand that, yes, some messed-up stuff happened. And because of that acknowledgment, I walked into deliverance and was spiritually healed from alcoholism. Today, I talk about my past freely and without fear or anxiety, because that's exactly what it is now, my past.

My testimony is simply that, what happened to me won't necessarily
happen to others. If you are an addict or know of an addict who is medicine dependent, doctor-dependent, and/or therapy-dependent, please work with the professionals to help you or your friend to full recovery. Always consult the professionals in your life.

If you wonder if you are an addict or are simply ready to quit, please research rehabilitation centers nearest to you. They will point you in the right direction. You can also seek pastoral counseling and find Christian rehabilitation centers online. Sometimes, talking to close friends and family will help as well. If you have any questions for me, please visit my blog page at **www.memorybengesa. com.** *Thanks!*

Acknowledgements

I thank God for the privilege of ministering in writing. I give Him all the glory, for my hands are mere tools used for Him. I am truly humbled to be a servant of my divine creator. It is truly through the divine that we are creators.

Memory Bengesa